RAF LINDIA

# A
# ONE WAY
# TICKET

*I love you because the entire universe
conspired to help me find you.*

*Paulo Coelho*

# Prologue

## University of California San Diego, 1995

Robert Lewis looked down from his dorm room window toward the campus lawn where his college graduation ceremony would later take place. He watched as the white plastic chairs were meticulously arranged in rows in front of the main stage, and all around the event attendants completed the final preparations.

Robert had loved his time at UC San Diego. He had studied hard but found plenty of time for campus activities throughout his college years. Driven by his passion for politics and writing, he had written for the university newspaper since freshman year. He had participated fervently in political debates organized by the various student associations, and gotten involved in various student movements.

When he wasn't studying or writing or trying to make change, he was with Patty. She was in the class behind him. They had met at a party on campus and from that first moment, they had become inseparable. They had immediately fallen in love and came to be each other's best friend. She was from San Diego and so she was still living with her parents. Robert was from the other side of the country, from Greenwich, Connecticut. They came from two entirely different social backgrounds. He was the son of a prominent lawyer, and she was the daughter of two high school teachers.

Robert and Patty met every night after class. They would study together or go to the movies or grab a bite to eat at the Surfside bar, a student hangout near the campus.

Patty liked to sit with him, sipping a beer and listening to his various political theories and opinions. Robert was always a volcano of ideas, opinions and stories.

He had the fervor of one who wanted to change the world, even though his true passion was writing stories. He dreamed that he could change the world through his stories. Stories with a strong moral that would shake the soul of the reader.

Patty was fully convinced that one day, Robert would succeed. She was convinced that Robert was one of those dreamers who would tenaciously fight to realize his dreams, no matter what it took.

This passion was one of the things she loved most about Robert.

As Robert's graduation had approached, the two of them had started talking more and more about their future and what they would do to make their dreams come true. Together.

Patty still had a year left and Robert had promised to wait for her. He would stay in San Diego to be close to Patty and start writing his first novel. When she graduated, the two would decide where to live and how to support themselves while they pursued their dreams.

She was planning to specialize in criminology or psychology. While Patty planned to become a university professor, her great passion was painting. And she dreamed of a life doing both.

But central to all of her dreams was to make them happen next to Robert.

What Patty didn't know was that Robert had begun to struggle with his decision. He had promised Patty he would stay with her in San Diego for her last year, but his parents did not approve. When he had told them that he was not going to law school the next fall, and that he planned to stay with Patty and work on his novel, his father had gone crazy.

Robert's parents were convinced that he had to establish a more certain future. More safe. And that the best path for him was to follow in his father's footsteps and become a lawyer. They had pushed him to take the law school admissions test and to apply to his father's alma mater, NYU School of Law, where, with his grades and his father's significant alumnus status, he had a good chance of getting in.

After months of fighting over it, his father had finally told him that if he did not follow the plan, they would cut him off financially, and he would be entirely on his own. Robert knew he was serious.

This pressure had been building for months, and now, on that monumental day, his graduation day, Robert was staring out the window at the campus lawn with the sadness of that choice being forced upon him, and even more so because he had not shared any of this with Patty.

He knew it was going be painful, but he had decided to do it that night. After the ceremony. After the celebrations. They would go to his room and he would tell her that it was breaking his heart, but that he had to leave for New York in a few days. That his father had made it impossible for him, and that all their plans would have to be set aside.

Robert worried it would be the end of their love story. They had often talked about it because they were one year apart, and he was East Coast while she was West Coast. Neither of them thought long distance relationships truly could work. And that is why they made the promise for the next year. They both knew that at their age, once separated by thousands of miles, their love wouldn't survive.

They'd known friends who tried to do it after graduation, living apart, but ultimately they all found themselves miserable, wondering what the other was doing, waiting by the phone or in front of the mailbox, and eventually moving on to face the distractions of their new life.

They were practical enough to know that a relationship like that could not last.

So that night, Robert would try to explain the reason for his decision. There was the pressure of his parents but also the awareness deep in some part of him that thought they were probably right, it was the only thing to do. The safer path, as his father had called it. Robert would tell her why he had no choice, and assure her that if their destiny was to be together, as they believed it to be, then they would come to be together again.

Robert sighed deeply and looked in the mirror one last time before leaving his room to meet up with his parents who had just arrived for the event.

***

Patty Dawn was still fixing her makeup sitting in her room when her father called from downstairs.

"Patty! If you don't hurry up we'll be late for the event! I know you don't want to miss the most important moment for Robert!"

The young woman looked at the alarm clock next to the bed.

"Shit. It's late." she whispered to herself.

Getting up, she looked in the mirror one last time. She had chosen a short olive green dress to wear that day. She knew Robert would like it. She smiled at herself, excited, and ran out of the room and down the stairs.

"Mom, Dad, are you ready?"

Her father stared at her with ironic eyes.

"Only for the last hour, I'd say. Come on, let's go."

Once all three settled into her parents' small hatchback they headed for the university campus a few miles away.

"Did you tell Robert about our decision?" Patty's father asked her, looking at her in the rearview mirror.

Patty was staring out the window distracted.

"Not yet. I want to surprise him after the ceremony. I know how stressed out he's been about how he's going to make ends meet next year. So I'm going to tell him about it tonight. I can't wait. He's going to be thrilled."

Mr Dawn smiled at his daughter then looked back at the slow traffic ahead.

Patty's parents had decided to retire from teaching that year and take a year to go traveling. The trip around the world they had always dreamed of and planned for the time of their retirement.

They would leave the house free and Robert could move in with Patty while she finished her senior year.

She couldn't wait to live with Robert. And he would use that year, as they had planned, to draft his first novel.

***

Mr. Dawn found parking not far from the ceremony area. Hundreds of people were pouring into the meadow to follow the graduation. Relatives dressed elegantly for the occasion mixed with young students proudly displaying their caps and gowns.

Patty tried to catch a glimpse of Robert in the crowd as she zigzagged between people, dragging her parents along until finally, out of impatience she just left them behind.

"Olive green? Are you trying to make someone go crazy with this sexy short dress, young lady?" a voice behind her said.

Patty turned around. Robert was smiling at her sheepishly, decked out in his graduation gown with the cap sitting precariously on the side of his head.

The girl hugged him tight.

"Yes, I am looking for the most handsome graduate of the Class of 1995. Could you point him out to me?"

Robert grabbed her around the waist and kissed her fully on the lips.

"This color looks great on you," he told her as he held her back to look at her.

"Wish I could say the same for you," she replied, laughing and gesturing at the young man's formal gown.

"I prefer you in jeans," she concluded, kissing him again.

Their parents arrived at that moment. It was the first time they were meeting. The four warmly shook hands.

While everyone was speaking cordially, Robert was pulled away by his father.

"I wanted to give this to you before the ceremony." he said as he pulled a white envelope out of his jacket pocket and handed it to his son.

Robert stared at the envelope as he took it.

"What is it, Dad?" asked the young man.

Mr. Lewis took a deep, proud breath.

"Here is your one-way ticket to JFK and the lease on a studio apartment near Washington Square Park, just a few steps from NYU campus. My gift for you, my son, for achieving this milestone and moving onto the next."
Robert could not tear his eyes away from the envelope in his hand. Without opening it.

And there it was. It was all decided. Planned.

From there, in a few days he would leave, five thousand miles away from the love of his life. Their plans, dreams, would all change.

And she had no idea this was coming.

Robert finally looked away from what was in his hand and smiled at his father.

"You will see, son. One day you will thank me. It is the best choice you could have made." Said the man as he turned his gaze to Patty, who was talking to their mothers.

"She is a very sweet girl and I can see that she is in love with you. If your love is to be a love forever, then you both will find a way. No matter what career choices you make. Trust me."

Robert also looked over at Patty. He took a deep breath. He feared that what his father said was not true. They would get lost in their own daily life separated by thousands of miles. They would meet someone else. They would seek to share their everyday life with a new face. A new body. Their shared interests and passions would change, become different, living in different worlds.

Robert's choice would be the end of their story.

As everything rushed around them on that campus lawn. Robert stared sadly at his girlfriend. Patty looked at him and smiled.

She noticed the envelope he was holding in his hand and approached.

"What is it, love? What did he give you?"

Robert fumbled with the hem of his gown so he could quickly slip the envelope into his pants pocket.

"Nothing, my little mosquito. It's a gift from my father. I'll tell you later."

Patty smiled and looked at Mr. Lewis.

"I'm sure it's something good. Robert must have made you so proud, graduating with honors."

Mr. Lewis smiled at her.

"Yes. And his career will be full of success."

***

After the graduation ceremony and after the dinner and all the festivities, Robert and Patty went up to his dorm room.

They both had news to share. But the mood of the two was different. Her joy and enthusiasm were far from his sadness and sorrow at the thought of having to break his promise, to tell her that everything had changed.

Once in the dormitory and while Patty was in the bathroom, Robert reached into his pocket and took out his father's envelope.

He looked at it again without opening it and slipped the envelope under his pillow.

Once out of the bathroom, Patty hugged him and kissed him passionately.

"I have some great news for you. Let's say it's my parents' graduation gift."

Robert stared at her with heavy eyes.

"I have something important to tell you too. But it can wait. You go first," the boy said wanting to postpone that tragic moment for as long as possible.

A flash of concern crossed Patty's face, but she went ahead anyway. She made him sit on the bed and knelt in front of him staring up at him with a happy smile that almost lit up her face.

"The good news is that my parents decided to retire from teaching this year."

"And?" Robert asked confused as he stroked her hair.

"And, they decided to take a trip to celebrate their retirement. A trip around the world. For a whole year."

"Beautiful. Good for them," said Robert still confused as to what the good news meant for them.

"And, they decided to leave us the house. For us. You can move in with me until I finish senior year."

The boy remained silent as if he had not understood what Patty was saying to him.

"Don't you see, Robert? This means you don't have to worry about supporting yourself here until I'm done. You don't have to pay rent or anything. Isn't this amazing?"

Robert sat so still, it was as if he was petrified. Patty was adding an important piece to build their relationship while he, shortly thereafter, was going to destroy it.

She saw their imminent future under one roof, sharing every night while he was about to tell her that, in a few short days, he would move thousands of miles away from her. Putting his career and a safe future before everything. Before their love.

As Patty stared at him expectantly, Robert felt himself dying inside. His chest contracting with pain, he struggled to breathe.

He slid his hand under the pillow. He grabbed the envelope that contained the airline ticket, and his lease on a new life. The envelope that would melt away the beautiful smile from Patty's face.

He stared at Patty, her face still illuminated by happiness in a way that, perhaps, he would never see again, so radiant and full of love. He squeezed the envelope tight in his hand, and at that moment, he felt he was about to split off a part of himself and lose it forever.

**I**

**New York City, 2018**

Robert sat at the oak desk in the studio of his Park Avenue apartment. He stared at the sealed orange envelope in his hand with a dull gaze, his mind faraway. Even though he hadn't put that much inside, it felt incredibly heavy. It held the weight of a lifetime, summarized in a few words on a few sheets of paper. He placed the envelope on the desk and grabbed a pen from the NYU penholder.

He wrote the name of the recipient on it, his hand shaky. It was a name he knew well, a name he had written thousands of times, although in that moment, it felt like the first time. Once it was addressed, he slipped the envelope into his jacket pocket and straightened his silk tie. He stared into the void for a few more seconds and then took stock of the surrounding room: the books arranged on the shelf next to him and the photos on the wall taken during various trips, where his wife and son posed alongside him with everlasting smiles. He swiveled his chair to the window and stood. He stuffed his hands in his pockets and gazed out toward the horizon, visible over the treetops of Central Park rising beyond the buildings across the street.

He considered his life and the choices he'd made—the ones he deemed right and those he counted as wrong— never knowing if he'd made the right choice. He thought about his career. About his son. He thought about New York, about how much he loved the city that never sleeps, where everything is possible. How much he had always loved it until that moment — until the day when he'd had to look at it differently.

Here, everything is allowed; everything can be forgiven. Because it's New York, where a mistake can turn into life experience, where your friends don't come from the set of a sitcom but are just regular people who suffer from solitude like many others, looking for each other in those few places that managed to remain untouched by the stress and routine of the ever-moving city.

Hypnotized by the fluttering of the doves on the window ledge of the building across the street, Robert heard his wife, Susan, calling him from the other room. "Darling, coffee is ready. Will you come drink it with me in the kitchen?"

He withdrew from his thoughts. "Coming!"

He sat on a stool across the kitchen counter from Susan, and the couple occupied themselves with the news on their smartphones while they sipped their coffee.

Without taking her eyes off her phone, Susan chuckled and said, "Still, when I think of Anna I start laughing."

"Embarrassing," Robert replied, "but comical at the same time."

The night before, their friend Anna had slipped on the steps of the Richard Rodgers Broadway Theater where they went to see *Hamilton*, producing a tragicomic thud that got the attention of nearly the entire audience.

"Luckily, the only thing she hurt was her pride. And that was dramatic enough" concluded Susan before taking another sip of coffee.

Robert only nodded in agreement. "I'll be a little late tonight, by the way," he said, his eyes still on his phone screen. "Can you take care of dinner?"

"Sure, I can," Susan replied. "How about fettuccine Alfredo?"

Robert nodded and tried to appear as present as possible, but his thoughts were on the letter in his pocket. About the consequences it would lead to. About what had made him write it, seal it, and address it. About what he was about to do and its irreversible outcome.

Once he finished his coffee, he rose, put his cup in the sink, looked at himself in the mirror near the entrance, and turned to his wife for a last time. As she did every morning, she walked him to the door, where she kissed him on the lips and wished him a good day.

Robert stared at her for a moment. She was still very beautiful. After all those years, except for a few wrinkles, her face had not changed. She was as attractive and sexy as she always had been. Her short, straight red hair gave her an intriguing look. He had been attracted to her from day one, to her smile, the way she laughed, and the mischievous look she gave him when she sought intimacy.

Still, for Robert, this kiss was different from any other they had given each other during all those years of life together. It was a bitter kiss. It felt forced. This wasn't their usual morning parting.

In the hallway, he called the elevator and looked back at his closed apartment door. When the elevator arrived, he stepped inside, pressed the ground-floor button, and slipped the other hand into his jacket pocket, withdrawing the orange letter. He stared at it through the whole twenty-four-floor descent.

When the doors opened, Robert walked to mailbox 24D, which was labeled with both his and Susan's names. He unlocked it, barely noticed the other mail waiting for them, put the letter inside, and closed it again. He took a deep breath, trying to calm the crazy beating of his heart, which raced so fast that he felt it pulsing in his ears.

"Good morning, Mr. Lewis."

The sudden voice startled him. It was the building doorman.

"Good morning, Marc."

"Is everything okay, Mr. Lewis?"

Robert released a sigh before answering. "Yes, everything is fine. Let's just say I have a busy day ahead of me."

The doorman walked toward the glass door leading out to the street. "Then I wish you the best of luck, Mr. Lewis."

Knowing that luck had nothing to do with it, Robert nodded and let the doorman open the door for him. He turned south down Park Avenue, heading for his office at Lexington and 59th Street. He often walked to work, thinking about his tasks for the day. Ten years earlier, he had finally left the large law firm that had trained him and opened his own business law practice that provided services to small- and medium-sized companies. After a few years of and a bumpy start, he had managed to get noticed by a couple of boutique investment banks. Now he had seventeen people on his payroll. From there, he began to grow and expand his practice, now earning fees that were often into the seven figures.

He crossed at the corner of Park Avenue and 58th Street and stopped for a few moments. His mind went back to the envelope he had left in his mailbox and what was in it.

He froze, suddenly realizing that what he had just done was a cowardly way to solve his problem, immature and totally wrong. No, this matter had to be approached differently. He should have taken everything head-on. He pivoted on his heel —

Turning on that street corner, he felt everything, all of life in New York City, drift into slow motion around him. In the instant it took to raise his foot to race back, everything seemed to suspend. People walking by froze, blouses and ties billowing like ghostly jellyfish in the slipstream of passing cars. Traffic signals hovered in the liminal shift from red to green. People hailing cabs on every corner stiffened mid-gesture, their arms stuck stationary above them like naked flagpoles. The motion of buses, cars, bicycles, and delivery trucks smeared together in a riot of colliding colors.

He had to go back and retrieve the letter before someone else found it. Before Susan found it. His foot struck the sidewalk, and everything went back to normal speed.

In a single instant, Robert could clearly see all the things in his life that had led him to that precise moment — every choice, every coincidence, every encounter, every single crossroads he had found himself at. He hung in limbo, simply observing without conscious thought.

***

Susan left the apartment ten minutes after Robert. She surveyed herself in the elevator mirror, admiring the dark Armani suit she had recently purchased. She remembered Robert loving it when he had seen her trying it on in the store. Sure, it was a little more expensive than what she usually spent on clothes to wear at work, but they could afford it.

As a child psychologist, Susan tried not to dress too fancy or too expensive, so as not to make the children's parents uncomfortable. She knew that many of them were having both financial and emotional problems, and she tried not to create too much of a social gap between herself and her patients' families. Nevertheless, she couldn't pass on this suit.

"Good morning, Dr. Lewis," said Marc, opening the Park Avenue door for her as she approached.

"Good morning, Marc. How are you doing today?"

"Very well, Doctor. Now, if you'll forgive me for saying so, I noticed you haven't retrieved your mail for a few days. Perhaps you would like me to bring it up to your apartment?"

"Thank you, Marc," she replied, turning toward the street. "That won't be necessary. I'll grab it when I get back this evening if you can have it ready."

"As you like, Doctor. Have a good day."

Reaching the street, Susan stepped up to the curb and hailed a cab.

Even though the rent for her studio office in Columbus Circle was quite expensive, she loved the view of Central Park from there. She loved beautiful things. Very expensive things. She expected these things. She had grown up in a wealthy family and had lived in Manhattan all her life. Robert's family had money as well, but they were self-made and had a different kind of practicality.

She had met Robert by chance, at a café in Union Square where he'd had an appointment with a colleague and she had gone to meet with a friend. Neither person they'd intended to meet had showed up, and they found themselves sitting across from each other at adjacent tables. Overhearing Susan's phone conversation, Robert had joked that, by funny coincidence, his meeting had been canceled as well. That's how it all had started. By accident.

A year later, they were living together, and when she found out she was pregnant a few months later, they decided to get married. In the beginning, they had some problems because of their social differences. Nevertheless, they always loved each other and managed to grow up, both in their relationship and in their careers. Overall, she felt content with her life choices.

## II

That evening, when Susan returned, Marc rushed to call the elevator.

"Good evening, Dr. Lewis. Here's your mail, as promised." He handed her the stack of mail.

"Good evening, Marc," she replied absentmindedly and flipped through the mail as she rode the elevator to the twenty-fourth floor. The elevator door opened, and Susan found herself face to face with her neighbor.

"Good evening, Susan. Are you done with another hard day's work?"

Carla Goldman was an attractive woman in her forties, and Susan considered her to be the nosiest and most indiscreet person in the building. A few years earlier, when she'd discovered that her husband was having an extramarital affair, Carla had divorced, an incident that had compromised her personality, the way she interacted with others, and her chances of starting another relationship.

Susan plastered on a smile. "Good evening, Carla. Yes, rather long and intense. Now I also have to cook for Robert, and it looks like he is going to be late again."

"Men," Carla sneered. "I remember when my ex said he was going to be late, when in reality he was fooling around with other women and—"

"I understand, Carla," Susan interjected. She grimaced as she nervously inserted the key in the lock of her apartment. "But Robert is not like that."

Carla did not have time to finish speaking; Susan disappeared behind the door and purposely slammed it closed.

Safe inside the apartment, Susan sighed, disappointed once again at the constant indelicacy of her neighbor. As a psychologist, Susan knew that Carla had not yet overcome the trauma of her failed marriage and was seeking the commiseration and cooperation from others. Her husband had betrayed her, and she could not find peace.

Robert, on the other hand, was a faithful man. He and Susan had been married for eighteen years. Their son, Brian, who was a freshman in college, was smart, honest, and kindhearted. In addition to the apartment on Park Avenue, they owned a cottage in the Hamptons, and enjoyed a well-rounded and semi-lavish lifestyle.

Both had been working a lot lately. Robert had been of great support during the most delicate moments in her career. Now that the situation had reversed, and it was he who was in need, she was keenly aware of how important it was to return the favor. Of course, they had their ups and downs too, but now they were happy. Weren't they?

Without having finished looking at all the mail, she placed the bundle of correspondence on a little table in the hall and took off her coat. A letter with an orange envelope fell onto the floor. She picked it up and stared it closely. The envelope had only her first name, no address. It had not been sent from a postal office. Someone must had slipped it through the mail slot that very day. And it looked like her husband's handwriting.

Confused, Susan opened it, wondering why Robert would have chosen to let her find the letter this that way. She immediately thought about a probable surprise, such as a gift or a love letter. But even though she was used to Robert's romantic gestures, she couldn't think of any anniversary. It was April. It had been two months since Valentine's Day, her birthday was in July, and their wedding anniversary was in November.

She slipped out of the envelope a sheet of paper marked with a few handwritten lines and a photograph.

She stared at that picture, feeling as if the ground had suddenly fallen from beneath her feet. She rested her back against the closed door and slid down until she was sitting on the parquet floor.

Unable to think clearly, she watched her pain solidify into the tears that soaked the letter. Her trembling hand couldn't stifle her moan, and she gazed at the photo through eyes blurred by grief and dismay.

She knew the image too well. She couldn't think. Her whole life now clung to those words and that picture. A time lost in memory. Something forgotten. The dark moment that had led to a crossroad. Somehow the past had managed to find its way back. A lingering glitch, lost in a yesterday, ready to break into her life and take over her destiny, leaving no room for any compassion, forgiveness, or mercy.

Susan knew exactly what that message meant. She was aware that everything was about to change. Robert had brought her back to that precise moment in life. He'd stirred up the whirlwind that sucked her in, calling on her to face the unsolved. As if history had remained crouched on a ledge, waiting for the right moment to return and reclaim its truth.

Susan braced herself and rose from the floor. The few minutes she'd spent on the cold tile felt like an eternity. She kicked off her shoes, and, with the letter still gripped between her fingers, she let herself sink into the sofa, staring blankly at nothing.

The sun was setting behind the skyscrapers, plunging the red sky into darkness. As always, the city lights remained the only saviors of the night.

She looked at her watch. It was seven o'clock. Robert was about to come home, and she was still sitting on the sofa and without having cooked anything; neither of them would have the desire or the strength to eat. She was not even going to take off the Armani suit and carefully hang it up. She would wait for him, and they would deal with the situation. They would talk and cry. They would hug and help each other. They would look each other in the eyes with compassion and get over it.

Over the years, they had managed to overcome difficult times more than once. They were going to get through it this time, too.

***

At nine o'clock, after two glasses of wine, Susan was still sitting on the sofa, the ingredients of the meal she had intended to cook untouched. Her overburdened mind had no spare room to worry about Robert's delay. She knew she could text or call him but didn't yet feel the need. Truth be told, she was afraid to hear his voice. She needed to address this in person.

She got up and, taking the glass of wine with her, went to the window that overlooked the city. From that spot, one could almost see the people sitting at their desks inside the MetLife Building. The distant lights atop the iconic Chrysler Building and Empire State Building cast themselves across the city on either side. Susan had always loved that view. It made her feel proud and accomplished. But this night, everything looked blurry and sad, as if rain had poured down the windowpane, blending shapes and lights together in an indistinguishable smear.

The sudden ringing of her phone, still lying on the floor next to her purse, diverted her thoughts. She picked it up and looked at its screen.

It was Brian, their son. A few months earlier, he had left for Yale University to begin his undergraduate studies. His intention was to go to law school, to follow in his father's footsteps.

"Hey Mom."

Susan cleared her throat before speaking. "How are you, sweetheart? Where are you?"

"I'm on campus. I tried to call Dad to ask him a favor, but it looks like his phone is off. Is he there with you?"

She steeled herself for a moment before answering, "No darling, he's not back yet. He told me this morning he would be late. Is there anything I can do to help?"

"It's not that urgent, I can wait. Tell him to give me a call when he gets back, if he's not too tired."

They quickly said goodbye, and Susan dropped on the sofa along with her phone. She obviously couldn't explain to Brian that there was also this letter. What his father had sent her concerned only the two of them—her and Robert. It was something they had to deal with before burying it in the past where it firmly belonged.

At 9:30, Robert still hadn't shown up. For the first time that evening, she worried and wondered where he could be. She tried his cell phone, and as Brian had mentioned, it seemed to be off. Robert's recorded voice asked her to leave a message. She hung up. She tried calling the landline at the office, but the phone just kept ringing. Not even his secretary answered—evidence that everybody had left. Her nervousness grew.

Susan concluded it all had to do with the orange envelope and the letter inside; there could be no other explanation. Like every morning, they had had coffee together, and, like every day, he had bid her goodbye with a sweet kiss on the lips. Like every morning, he had asked her how she had slept. They had laughed in the mirror, talking about the night before, about Anna and her slip on the stairs of the theater. It could have been a day just like any other they'd had in the past few years. It seemed as if nothing could surprise them. As though nothing bad could have happened.

Robert had left the apartment shortly before her. He had probably posted that letter prior to leaving the building and then disappeared for the rest of the day.

But it had been no ordinary day after all. It had not been a morning like any other. Robert had had a plan. He'd had it for days, maybe weeks. He had asked her to take care of dinner. Everything suggested he would be back. If it hadn't been for the letter, and what she knew she would have to face.

Perhaps Robert needed some time to refresh his mind. To spend some time alone before the inevitable confrontation. In that moment, he was probably wandering around the city, meditating on what to do. About what they should say to each other. How they could solve the problem.

It was almost ten o'clock when her cell phone rang again. Susan didn't recognize the number on the screen. She answered.

Robert woke to the roaring of waves breaking against rocks. He remained still in bed a moment, listening to the synchronized and repetitive movement of the ocean. Drowsy, he pushed himself up and stalled, peering at the blue sheets. He didn't recognize them. He gazed toward the window overlooking the blue sea and the sky.

He got out of bed and looked around the room. Everything was unfamiliar: the furniture, the objects on the nightstands, and the photo of him and a woman sitting atop the dresser across from him. He knew the woman, but he hadn't seen her in years. He couldn't tell when the picture was taken, and he couldn't remember taking it.

He stopped to absorb the sweeping view from the window. From there he could see the waves overlapping, one on top of the other, as far as the eye could see, until they got lost in one another toward the horizon. People wandered among the rocks along the shoreline, where seagulls shuttled between the beach and the open sea, and a group of surfers straddled boards in the distance, waiting for the perfect wave to push them, surging and unrestrained, back to shore.

He focused on his reflection in the window glass. He wore only pajama pants. He recognized his graying hair, his lean body, his hairless chest, and green eyes. He spread his hands, studying them. Nothing about him had changed. He just didn't know where he was.

The shadows of palm trees, the seagulls, and the natural scenery of the beach were more reminiscent of the Pacific coast than the flat, sad Atlantic coastline. Lifeguard towers lined up one after the other on the long shoreline, which made him think of some California resort.

He suddenly felt dizzy and sat down on the unmade bed. He tried, without success, to remember how he ended up sleeping here in the first place. He then attempted to reconstruct the night before. Nothing came to him. He knew that he was not living there, for sure, but at the same time, he had no idea where his home was.

He knew who he was: Robert Lewis. The woman in the picture stared at him from the top of the dresser. Someone he could recognize. This place felt familiar, despite the fact he couldn't recognize the space and the objects in it. Was it someplace he used to live?

In that moment, he heard the door handle turn. He watched as the door slowly opened, and the woman in the photograph materialized on the threshold, holding a small tray bearing two cups of coffee. She had the same smile and the same black curls falling on her shoulders. She was wearing only a short white silk robe, and by the way it hugged the curves of her body, Robert was sure she wore nothing underneath.

Looking happy to see him awake on the bed, she smiled. Although he had remembered her differently, he recognized her. From a different world, a different time, at another age.

"Patty?!" he exclaimed with surprise.

Patty made an amusing grimace that failed to hide her disappointment. "Were you hoping some other woman would join you in bed with coffee, my love?" she replied with a laugh.

Robert watched her suspiciously as she approached. She placed the tray on the nightstand next to him and gave him a winking smile. "You'd better drink your coffee now. Otherwise, it will be too cold afterwards," she suggested as she dropped her robe, revealing her naked body.

She sat on his lap, handed him a cup, and watched as he slowly sipped the coffee. Though he was bewildered, he felt as if there was something familiar about it, as if nothing new was happening. Perhaps this was the life he had led up until the moment he'd lost himself. He just couldn't remember.

Patty waited for him to put the cup back on the bedside table and kissed him gently. Still smiling, she ran her hands through his hair.

"Patty, wait . . ."

She stopped just for a brief instant and smiled mischievously. "Why wait? Today I feel a strange energy inside of me. I just want to share it with you," she concluded, touching her lips to his chest.

***

Shortly afterward, Robert lay naked in bed while Patty took a shower. They had made love intensely. Although his emotional connection to her was strong, he couldn't, for the life of him, understand how he had ended up in that bed with his ex-girlfriend. Patty had been his first love. He knew her mostly by the shining smile that radiated from her beautiful face.

He remembered when she was young. Their love had begun in college, he was a sophomore and she was a freshman. Strong, intense, and pure, it had ended when he decided to change his plans and move to New York. No matter how much he wracked his brain for what came after, that was all he could remember. As he listened to the endless sound of the waves beyond the window, he became increasingly concerned that something, some kind of trauma, had made him lose his memory. Either that or he was going crazy.

He realized he should consult with Patty as soon as she was finished in the bathroom. Perhaps he should have done that prior to making love, he chided himself, but then he gave himself a break, realizing that his faculties weren't what they should be.

He could hear the water running in the shower. He forced himself to remember more. He just couldn't visualize anything that had happened in the previous days of his life. He had no idea what he did for a living. He couldn't even imagine what city he was in at that moment. He had entered the void.

He could clearly remember his childhood, his teenage years and then his studies of political science in college before deciding to pursue law. He wondered if he was an attorney perhaps, but it didn't jog a memory. He remembered his intense love for Patty. He thought back to all the Christmases spent with his parents and his sister, sitting around a festive table laughing and talking. He remembered the house where he grew up in Greenwich and canoeing on the Mianus River.

The curtains Patty had closed before they'd made love cast the room in a dim light. Lost, he struggled to reflect on what might have happened for him to lose his most recent memories. He alarmingly concluded that maybe he had brain cancer. He knew that type of pathology could commonly cause a sectional memory loss; he had studied it in his college days. Something had happened the previous night—a trauma. But he felt fine, he had no pain, and Patty didn't seem concerned about his health.

When she reappeared in the room wearing her fluffy purple bathrobe, Robert was still curled up in the sheets. "The shower is all yours, my love."

He turned to her and said in a strained voice, "We need to talk."

She stopped toweling her hair and stared at him. "Is something wrong?"

He sat up in bed and stared down at the sheets. "Yes, something's wrong with my memory. I'm really confused. I feel lost."

Patty quickly sat beside him, staring at him with anxious eyes. "What do you mean? What are you feeling, my love?"

He finally looked up at her, then shifted his gaze to the ceiling as if searching for the more appropriate or accurate answer to give her. "I woke up without knowing where I was. Actually, I still don't know where I am. I don't recognize this room. What house are we in? Which city? I know you, but I don't know what we are doing here now, together. Are we married? Do we have children? The only things I can remember are my childhood and our college days." He looked at the picture standing on the dresser. "I don't even remember when that picture was taken. Nothing."

Patty was silent for a few moments, terror and dismay plain on her face. "Tell me this is a joke. This isn't funny, Robert. I'm not enjoying it at all."

He sighed and clutched her hand. "No, Patty, it's not a joke."

"You did look a little confused when I walked in with the coffee," she admitted.

He stared blankly at her. "I was still trying to figure out where I was when you came in. I mean . . . I know who you are, but I don't remember us being together after that first year of college. I've completely forgotten our wedding, our days as husband and wife."

"You're *really* not kidding, are you?" Patty threw her arms around him. "Let's go see Dr. Paterson right now," she said, pulling back to peer worriedly into his eyes. "He will find an explanation for this. You may have had a trauma and didn't realize it."

"I was considering it, too . . . I mean, is there something you can think of that might have caused it? It must have happened last night. Is there anything that comes to mind?"

Patty got out of bed and paced back and forth. "Not really. We had dinner, drank a bottle of wine watching *Blind Spot,* and joked around. We laughed. Nothing different from the usual. We went to bed feeling peaceful, and, as we have been doing for years, we fell asleep hand in hand."

As he listened, Robert tried to visualize what she had described, hoping to recover the memory of those emotions. But nothing happened. He didn't even remember the shows she said they'd watched. "Do we have children? Does anyone else live in the house with us? Do we have a dog or other pets?"

Patty lowered her eyes. "No. We couldn't have children, and no, we don't have a dog, but you've been talking about it."

"What do I do for a living?" Robert asked.

With a sudden smile of appreciation and pride, she looked up at him again. "You are a world-renowned writer. Your six novels have been translated into sixteen languages. Don't you remember that, either?" She squeezed his hand. "You are so proud of your accomplishments. We both are."

Robert felt a thrill shoot through him. Being a writer had been his dream since he was a child, that he could remember. He had initially chosen to study philosophy for that reason before changing his mind, having realized it was too risky. He did remember collaborating with the editors of the school newspaper. As a freshman in college and being politically active, he had even written speeches for classmates running in college elections.

"Six novels, huh? What are they about?"

With a creased brow, Patty said without a hint of condensation, "You write in various genres—adventure/romance, espionage, and a couple of thrillers."

They fell into a moment of silence before Patty stood up. "Let's not waste time and go see Dr. Paterson. We have to figure out what happened to your memory."

"Right now?" Robert asked with surprise, though he knew it was the best course of action. "What's today?"

"Wow," she said with concern. "You don't even remember the day?"

Robert shook his head.

"It's Saturday. When Dr. Paterson hears it's you, he won't have any problem seeing you today."

Robert wondered who this Dr. Paterson was and why he had such sway over a doctor's attention, but he went through the motions of getting ready in unfamiliar clothing that fit like a glove. Before they left, he thumbed through the novels he'd apparently written; not even the covers looked familiar. He wanted to feel pride but felt nothing.

With his nerves on edge, Robert rose from the table when Dr. Paterson retracted it from the CT scanner. He took a small chair beside Patty, expecting to hear the worst, in front of the doctor's desk while he examined the results. For some endless minutes, Robert and Patty held hands and waited.

After a careful examination of the data and scans, Paterson looked at them with visible agitation. "Mr. Lewis, I'm afraid I'm not able to give you an explanation," said the doctor, waving the papers in his hands. "There seems to be nothing pathological from a neurological point of view. I can't see any evidence of trauma or tumor and can't detect any foreign body or malformation in your brain."

"Well, that's comforting," Robert said with relief. "But then why this amnesia?"

Dr. Paterson slumped back in his chair and clasped his hands. "It isn't unheard of for a person to lose their memory following an accident, after brain surgery, or upon awakening from a coma. But none of those things pertain to you. If you want, I could do some more diagnostic tests, but at this point, what I know of your case makes me think more of a psychological cause than a physical or neurological one."

Patty leaned forward. "So, you think what's keeping Robert from regaining his memories is a *mental* disorder?" she asked apprehensively.

Paterson pondered for a few seconds. "Yes, it's possible that something external triggered an old latent trauma and his mind, as if in a kind of self-defense, caused him to have this memory loss."

Robert searched his brain for some forgotten childhood trauma and came up with nothing. "Is it going to be temporary or permanent?" he asked, trying to keep his emotions in check.

"It's hard to tell," Dr. Paterson replied after a moment. "Usually, this type of amnesia can be resolved. There are multiple factors that can help in a recovery, but it's difficult to predict how long it will take."

"What kind of factors?" Patty asked hopefully.

"Memory exercises, encouragement from loved ones, living in familiar places, and even a daily routine. Meditation perhaps. Music. These are all things that help speed up recovery time, whether it's full or partial. It's hard to quantify, though," replied the doctor, visibly distraught at not being able to give more precise information. "I'm going to ask my assistant to give you the name of a psychologist who will be able to help you in your recovery."

Robert and Patty sought comfort in each other's eyes. The mind was still an unexplored field, even from a doctor's point of view, and this alarmed Robert. However, it was true that, in many cases, the right motivation would be enough to bring the foggy part of the brain back on track. He would do everything he could to recover what, for some unknown reason, had been lost.

Terrified, Patty considered how Robert felt in this moment of darkness, fear, and uncertainty. She imagined it would be like standing in a dark room, unable to find the light switch or the way out. She gazed at her husband, feeling as if he were an empty shell—a body devoid of the essence of her man. Anguished, she couldn't stop wondering what sort of trauma could have caused such damage to his mind.

Once out of the hospital, Patty got behind the wheel of their Range Rover, wondering if Robert could remember the way home. Did he still know how to drive? Impulsively, she pulled into a parking lot behind a mall, swerving haphazardly, and stopped the car in the middle of the half-empty lot.

"Why did you stop?" asked Robert, who had remained silent until then.

"I want to see if you remember how to drive," she replied as she unbuckled her seat belt and opened the door. She didn't feel any amusement at their predicament and was doing everything she could to hold herself together.

Robert got behind the wheel. He started the car and drove off with hesitation. Patty noticed he drove smoothly, as he always did. Maybe sometimes he was a little too aggressive with the accelerator. As always, he was distracted by all the road signs. What he couldn't do, however, was find his way home. She had to give him the directions.

"So far we found out that you remember how to drive. You remember me when I was young. You didn't forget about your childhood. Do you by any chance remember any of your friends?"

Discouraged, Robert shook his head no. "A few guys, back in college."

"Well, today you have a bunch of new friends. You met them when we settled here, in Laguna Beach."

"*Why* do we live here in Laguna? And where did we move from?"

Patty sighed and began with trepidation but soon realized she enjoyed recounting and reliving the things they had done together. It intrigued her to see how her husband, with the eyes and the mind of a stranger, would judge everything she would remind him of about their lives for who knew how many days to come.

"After college, I studied criminology and eventually got a teaching position at UCLA," she began. "You came with me to LA, but you were still struggling as a writer. You had written a short thriller that was rejected by all the publishers you contacted. You wanted to succeed right away and felt frustrated."

"Then why do I recall heading to New York by myself after graduation?"

Robert interjected. "We broke up."

Patty looked at him quizzically. She wondered how her husband could have such a distorted memory when he couldn't remember anything else. "I don't know—you considered moving to New York but decided to stay. Your father was pressuring you to be practical and go to law school. He even threatened to stop supporting you financially. But you decided to follow your dreams, and in the end, you were right. You became what you always wanted to be. A published author, and a very successful one.

"Although you never clearly said that you gave up on New York for me—I guess because you didn't want me to feel responsible—I really think you did it to be close to me. When we moved to LA, we rented a studio apartment in Hollywood. You kept writing, hoping to fulfill your dream to be published, and I went to teach classes every morning.

"At first, it was difficult to live in the city on my salary alone. Until the day a publisher picked up your first novel, the story of a man who finds an heirloom and discovers its connection to a broken love. The book had a happy ending. The two lovers, thanks to this object, managed to find each other again and lived the rest of their lives together. A beautiful love story, but also with some action. It was published shortly thereafter by one of New York's top publishing houses. From that moment on, our lives changed considerably."

"What do you mean?" Robert asked, following Patty's directions to the front of their house. He was enjoying her story, but that's all it was to him: a story.

"You started traveling a lot. You left for a book signing and meet-the-author tour. You were making a lot of money and we were able to move to a bigger apartment. We were living the dream. But from that day on, and book after book, success slowly became too much for us. So, after seven years in LA, we decided to find a place where we could be out of the spotlight. Some place warm and not too far from a major airport or a major metropolis, in case we got bored."

"And did we ever get bored?" Robert asked as they got out of the car.

Patty stopped him in the doorway of the villa, took his hand, and looked him square in the eyes. "No. On the contrary. We began to enjoy our life outside the city. We met interesting and friendly people. In New York, we were always by ourselves. Because that's a city where one can have hundreds of friends and still feel alone. Even right in the middle of a crowd. Today, we have our own routine. Every Saturday night, you meet your friends at the bar, while I have dinner with their wives on our terrace, since it has such a gorgeous view of the ocean. We both enjoy the same TV shows, and every two or three months, we take off for a brief vacation, each time to a different place in the world. I don't teach anymore, but I do research. You've been writing less in these days, so we have more time to spend doing the things we like together: art, music, trips, and theater . . ."

"Why didn't we have children?" Robert asked for the second time that day, as they entered the house. They went to sit on the terrace, where they could see the rush of the sea below them.

Patty sighed before replying. "We couldn't. We did so many tests! There is nothing wrong with us. Sometimes it happens. Some people, for chemical or physical reasons, can't procreate. We thought about adopting once but changed our minds."

Robert felt the stirrings of disappointment and distracted himself with his sudden thirst. He stood up, and Patty followed him into the kitchen.

"What do I usually drink at this time of day?" he asked, eying the Brooklyn Lager on the refrigerator shelf.

She smiled. "You like to sip a cold beer, but only on weekends. During the week, you like to work out a little. At night, we drink wine."

Robert grabbed the beer, and Patty retrieved a can of bubbly water before returning to their seats.

The cold beer felt comforting in Robert's hands. He gestured a toast toward the horizon. "Do we love each other?"

She smiled again. "Yes. We do love each other very much. Let's say we complement each other. We've never, or at least not yet, gotten tired of each other, our sex . . . we rarely fight, even though sometimes I get angry at your stubbornness."

Robert turned to her and genuinely smiled for the first time since they'd returned from the doctor's appointment.

"Can I ask *you* a question now?" asked Patty.

"Of course," he responded.

"Did you enjoy making love to me this morning?" she asked with a hint of embarrassment.

Robert stared into her eyes. "Yes," he replied. "It was intense and deep. There I was, a guy with no memory and in total shock. In an instant, you pushed those frightening thoughts away. You should have noticed how much I enjoyed it." He took a sip of his beer.

Patty let go of the breath she'd been holding. "By the way, on Saturday nights, you have your usual date at the bar with your friends—*David, Steve,* and *John.*" She looked at him to see if the names rang a bell.

"David, Steve, and John, huh?" Robert said. "I got nothing."

Patty sighed. "Anyway, it will be a great opportunity to try to jog your memory."

Robert lowered his gaze to the wooden deck. "I wouldn't even know how to recognize them, much less figure out where the bar is."

"I'll call our friends and explain the situation," she assured him. "One of the guys will pick you up, and you can all try to fill the void together. Your friends think very highly of you. I'm sure they are going to be very understanding and helpful."

Robert wasn't sure how he felt about hanging around with guys he couldn't remember, but he knew it would at least be a starting point to begin piecing his life back together.

## V

The sappy jingling of the doorbell broke Robert's attention from the meticulously organized master bedroom closet.

Patty called from the hallway. "John's here!"

He attempted to conjure an image of John in his mind but couldn't. It jangled his nerves even more. He tried to convince himself that tonight's plans could help him solve this absurd situation. He trusted Patty. Visual stimulation would be essential for the recovery of his memories. But he was also exhausted from the crazy day of wracking his brain and coming up with no recent memories other than those he'd made that day. Patty's long account of their life together hadn't shed any light on that darkness.

Robert sighed and tried to muster up some courage. It would take time to unravel the issue. Or maybe the ordeal would vanish after a good night's sleep. He grabbed a white shirt and put it on over a pair of jeans and sneakers, hoping that that was the way he usually dressed for "boys" night.

He walked down the stairs. A man who looked to be in his forties waited for him in the kitchen, where Patty was busily assembling a charcuterie board for the friends she'd be hosting that evening. He was about Robert's height, six feet, only he had a bit of a belly that suggested he often kept company with a few good beers.

"Hey, man!" exclaimed the man with a wince of embarrassment.

"You must be John," Robert replied with a friendly but uncertain smile.

The man burst into thunderous laughter. "That's me! One of your best friends. I think *the* best, actually," he said turning his gaze to Patty, who seemed equally as embarrassed and amused by the unusual moment.

"Without the shadow of a doubt!" Patty confirmed with a smile, clutching her husband's arm.

At Patty's affectionate gesture, for the first time that day, Robert seriously considered how difficult this situation must be for her, too. He turned to her and kissed her softly.

She smiled, as if she had read his mind. "Thank you, my love. You might not remember it, but you're still tender and sweet."

***

On the short ride to The Cliff restaurant in John's Mustang convertible, Robert admired the breathtaking view of the thin horizon separating the cobalt sea from the blue of a clear Californian sky, by the waves, the beach, and the jagged coastline. Then his thoughts went back to what lay ahead. To Patty and his friends, this night out could be a simple habit. But what for everyone else was yet another outing among friends was a novelty to Robert. He would be spending the evening in an unknown place, having drinks with equally unknown people.

As he drove, John visibly struggled to be as friendly and detailed as possible, as if trying to make sure Robert could understand what he was talking about. Instead, Robert couldn't understand a thing of what John was talking about. Not only because he was jumping from one topic to another, but also because of the noise of the wind whizzing by over the open roof of the car.

Robert decided to say nothing and lost himself in the confusion of his thoughts. How long would he go on not remembering, and when would he get back to being normal, back to that life that Patty had described so well and which to him sounded so perfect?

***

David and Steve leaned on David's car in the parking lot of The Cliff, both feeling trepidation at what was about to unfold. The shiny black Ferrari that pulled into a spot near David's car momentarily caught their attention and admiration. They watched a man in his late seventies step out of the vehicle. He looked like a typical wealthy, eccentric Californian senior, with a khaki shirt over linen pants and a white hat with a wide visor. He nodded at the men, opened the hood, and started to arrange something in the front trunk space. The men turned their attention back to each other.

"Honestly, when Patty called to say that Robert woke up with no memory, I thought it was some crazy hoax they were playing on us," David said, resuming their earlier conversation. "I realized I'd never heard her sound so desperate. Rachel and I talked it over, and we don't think it's a joke."

"Neither do Sarah and I. The crazy part," Steve added, "is that he still has memories from over twenty years ago. With amnesia, don't you pretty much forget everything? And isn't there usually a cause?"

"It's not like anything has happened to him recently that would wipe his memory," David commented. "Plus, he's been enormously successful. What trauma could there be in that?"

They both turned to look at the old man as he closed the hood of his Ferrari. He waved at them with a peculiar expression on his face and walked toward the entrance of the club.

They watched as Steve and Robert pulled in and went over to greet their lost friend.

***

Neither David nor Steve evoked any meaningful memories in Robert's mind. Both gray-haired and massively built, they looked so alike that they could easily be mistaken for brothers.

The two men hugged Robert affectionately after awkwardly introducing themselves, for a second time, to their friend. Though they tried, they were unable to mask their concern.

"So, Robert, what the hell is going on with you?" asked David as he made the way to their usual table with a view.

Robert didn't reply.

John pointed Robert to the seat by the railing. "You always sit here so that you can look at the ocean all the way down to Dana Point," he said sheepishly.

Robert smiled at him and perched in the chair where he sat captivated, almost enraptured, by the colors of the vast landscape behind the railing. The sunset made the view even more spectacular, splashing crimson across the waves all the way to the beach.

David and Steven sat at the other side of the table, and John took the seat next to him.

"So, buddy," David said, "Patty filled us in on the temporary amnesia, but I want to hear it from your point of view. So let me ask again: What's going on?"

Robert looked away from the sunset and met David's inquisitive stare. "It's like my memory of the last twenty years has literally been erased. Nothing. I don't remember you guys. I don't remember writing my books, getting married, moving here . . . Like I said, nothing."

He had his friends' rapt attention.

"It's disconcerting, to say the least. I *want* to remember, but I just can't. It's like trying to solve a puzzle with your eyes closed. So damn frustrating." Robert shifted in his seat, feeling heat rising to his face.

"Patty says the doctor recommends stimulating your memory," Steve said, speaking at last, "by trying to retrace our habits together. But wouldn't it be better if you were in the hospital? It could be something serious."

The other two echoed Steve's sentiments.

"I spent several hours this morning in Dr. Paterson's office at Newport Hospital," Robert replied calmly, trying to reassure himself as much as his friends. "He's a friend, or so Patty tells me. Nothing neurological came up. I'm meeting with a therapist tomorrow to determine if there's a psychological aspect of this. I don't want to do any more tests. I am sure this is only temporary, some sort of blackout. Perhaps a childhood trauma somehow resurfaced and created this temporary void. Both Patty and the doctor suggested I come here with you guys, see if this could help me remember."

His friends exchanged worried glances.

"I'll be better tomorrow," Robert concluded, not quite convinced himself, and lowered his eyes to the menu.

Silently, the four men studied the various choices recommended by the restaurant that week.

"What do I usually order?" asked Robert with a smile, attempting to break the awkward silence.

"You like seafood," John answered promptly. "Salmon or shrimp are usually your go-tos. You drink wine. Strictly white and as dry as possible."

Robert gave his friend a quick nod of appreciation before going back to his menu.

"How is Patty handling all this?" asked David, bringing everyone's attention back to the topic of the night.

Robert hesitated. "I guess she's terrified, but she tries not to show it. Right now, given the situation, you know her better than I do. I know she's scared. I can hear it in her voice, see it in her eyes."

The other three nodded. Robert knew that Patty had made them aware of how delicate the situation was and how difficult it was to try to make things appear normal when there was nothing normal at all going on.

As he spoke, Robert felt someone watching him. He glanced several times over to the bar and saw an older clean-shaven gentleman staring at him. At first, he thought he might be a local or maybe someone just retired from some prestigious firm in New York or Los Angeles. When Robert met his eyes, the man raised his martini and smiled.

Just then, the waiter arrived to take their orders. Robert ignored the stranger's gesture and ordered grilled salmon, a baked potato, and a glass of Pinot Grigio.

As the evening progressed, Robert laughed genuinely as his friends recounted the most comical moments they had apparently experienced together, hoping that a detail might give him a foothold to regain his memory. He enjoyed hearing all the times he'd found himself in ridiculous situations. He tried to identify with his own character, but nothing clicked.

The more he listened to stories he couldn't remember, the more frustration he felt. At this point he knew he was the author of several best sellers. He was married to a beautiful woman who apparently loved him as much now as she had when they were first together. They had no children because of some divine will. He had wealthy friends who had each found success in their respective careers. He himself was probably very wealthy, although he couldn't didn't know how much he owned. He had an oceanfront mansion with a breathtaking view. He had a couple of sport cars in the garage and a collection of old watches that had to be worth a fortune, which were kept in the walk-in closet in the bedroom. He had no pets and had been living in Laguna Beach for the last decade. He had previously been based in LA for seven years where, after a period of hardship, he had achieved success with his first novel. Nothing else. He thought he should have asked Patty where his family was and if his parents were still alive.

But maybe there would be no need for it. Maybe, the next morning, he would wake up remembering his past. Everything that happened that day would remain just a terrible nightmare, a detour in his seemingly perfect life . . .

He would hug his wife, and they would make love again. This time, he would recognize her and remember how to satisfy her. They would have coffee, like every morning of all those years together, and they would laugh at the thought of what had happened. They would appreciate more who they were and life itself. They would not take anything for granted.

These hopes crowded Robert's mind even when, after calling it a night, John drove him back to Patty among awkward silence. The only light on in the house was the one in the bedroom. Patty's friends must have already left, and she was waiting up for him. It was almost eleven o'clock.

When Robert entered the room, Patty, who until then had been absentmindedly reading a book, got out of bed and ran to hug him. "How did it go, my love?" she asked.

Robert began to undress. "Good. They're nice people, and I feel like they sincerely care about me."

"Anything come back to you?"

He lowered his eyes. "They tried their best. They told me all the things we did together. I don't remember a stitch of it."

Patty hugged him again, more tightly. "Don't be afraid. Everything will go back to normal soon. Tomorrow we'll go to your session with Dr. Foster, and we'll see what she recommends."

Robert sighed. For the first time since that morning, he felt unsafe and terrified, like an alien living in a stranger's body. Empty and without a past, he felt like he'd been thrown into the deep end of a pool but didn't know how to swim.

As he stood clasped in the arms of the woman he only remembered as his first love, he gazed at their loving embrace reflected in the mirror. They were both in their late forties. His last memories of them dated back more than twenty years, when they were two young people in love excited about life. Now, by some cruel game of fate, they were still close, but without each other.

Robert couldn't wait to find himself again, to get back to who he had been. His thoughts spun in a mind without memories, empty and useless, little more than a dark room. All he had were blurry images of decades earlier and nothing else. Better he should try to sleep with the hope that, the next morning, everything would be back to where it should be. Everything would be back to normal. All the rest would have been only a terrible nightmare.

**VI**

Robert plunged headlong into a surreal dream as soon as his head hit the pillow that night. He stood at a traffic light with hundreds of people around him. Car horns echoed in his head. The voices of passersby were so amplified they drowned each other out into an incomprehensible din. In a trance, he watched the flashing hand of the pedestrian indicator, instructing him to wait before crossing.

Waiting on the same side of the road, next to him, a homeless man, swore incomprehensibly into the void. The man reeked, such a filthy smell that Robert could barely keep from throwing up. He moved a few steps away and found himself in the middle of the street, trapped between the cabs and the cars speeding in both directions.

Despite his deep sleep, Robert twitched. He found himself in a room, sitting in front of a tearful young man. Although he did not recognize him, he felt a deep affection for him. In seeing him cry, Robert felt connected with his suffering. He stretched out his hand, but the boy ignored him and continued to sob.

Robert tried in vain to get the boy's attention. He twitched again in bed as his dream state thrust him into a different darkness, where a beautiful woman with heavy eyes pulled him by his arm and begged him to follow her. Robert struggled to free himself from her strong grip. Displeased, the woman showed a gloomy sneer through pouty lips disheveled by smudged lipstick. She seemed to notice his bewilderment then and quickly closed her lips, forcing a smile.

At that moment he opened his eyes and saw Patty sitting against the headboard, gently stroking his forehead.

"My love, it was just a nightmare. I'm right here. Don't be afraid." Her expression was serene, but a tear slipped down her cheek.

Robert looked at her for a long time. Although he couldn't remember everything he'd experienced with her, he felt love. It was the only certainty he had in that moment. Even if he couldn't clearly remember those last years, he knew that a strong feeling must have bonded them for quite some time. There was a certain familiarity that not even the weird trick his mind was playing on him could conceal. He curled up in Patty's arms and closed his eyes, pondering the meaning of the dreams. The traffic lights. The young man in tears. The woman with the smudged lipstick.

Did all those images have something to do with his loss of memory? He knew, or at least had always believed, that dreams were fragments of real life, thoughts, or casual situations. A sort of psychic garbage, trashed by the brain during the night to restore the mind after a long day. Sometimes they were remembered upon waking; sometimes they weren't.

But on that specific night, everything could have been related to his mental state. Everything could be used to understand what was happening to his memory. Everything could have made sense. A few minutes more and Robert sank back into sleep, lulled by Patty's sweet caresses.

"I love you, Patty," he whispered as he closed his eyes.

"I love you too," she murmured, her voice choked with emotion. "So very much."

***

Robert left Patty sitting in the waiting room and entered Dr. Foster's office. Dr. Foster was an attractive and elegant woman in her late fifties with a bright smile. They sat in high-backed chairs with a coffee table between them, in the middle of which stood a box of Kleenex. Looking at it, Robert imagined Foster's patients having emotional outbreaks, having let go of the miseries and limitations of their existences. He realized in that instant that he had forgotten to ask Patty if he had ever been in therapy before.

"Mr. Lewis," said the doctor, smiling sweetly, "first I want to tell you that it's an honor to make your acquaintance. I have had the pleasure of reading all your novels."

"Thank you," he replied, "even if right now, as you know, it's impossible for me to remember any of them. And thank you for seeing me on a Sunday."

"As I told you, it's an honor," Dr. Foster insisted. She opened her notepad. "Now, let's think about how I can help you. First of all, tell me what happened when you woke up the other morning."

Robert lowered his gaze to the small coffee table and recounted every single detail he had experienced since waking up the morning before, from the confusion he felt as soon as he opened his eyes to the intimacy he'd shared with Patty, from what Dr. Paterson had told him to the night out with his friends. Nothing and no one he had met during that day had managed to awaken his memories. He even told her about the dreams he had the night before.

Throughout, Foster took copious notes, her eyes darting between her notepad and Robert's face.

"I feel it is important that you know that the only person I remember is my wife. But not at her actual age. I remember her when she was young, back in our college days."

"What is your last memory with her?" Dr. Foster inquired.

Robert paused a few moments before answering. "I remember the day I left. I was at the airport, waiting for the flight to New York. A flight that, according to Patty, I never took. While in my memory, I did take it. I even said goodbye to her. I knew that the long distance would not have helped the relationship, so we had . . . actually, I had decided that it was better to end it there." He stopped, overcome with a wave of grief. "In my mind, it's as if I haven't seen her since that day."

"What do you mean?" Dr. Forster asked, intrigued.

"When I saw her walk into the room yesterday, the first thing I thought was that it was the same woman in the picture on the dresser in our bedroom. It didn't occur to me that I lived with her."

Dr. Foster continued to take notes. Robert watched her intently, hoping to spot a grimace or an expression that could reveal her thoughts about his case.

"One last question, Mr. Lewis," she said from behind her notepad. "Do you have any difficulty remembering the events of the yesterday and this morning, or do you have them all clearly in mind?"

"I remember everything very well," he affirmed.

A brief but equally meaningful silence followed. After taking a few final notes, Dr. Forster let out a deep breath. "Okay, Mr. Lewis. Now, would you mind if I spoke with your wife for a few minutes?"

"Not at all," he said as he stood.

***

Patty waited anxiously as Dr. Foster reviewed her notes. When she looked up at Patty, she sighed and broke the silence. "I can only imagine how difficult these last twenty-four hours must have been for you."

Patty lowered her gaze to her hands, clasped in her lap. "A real nightmare. The night before, our life was perfect, and today my husband doesn't remember the hundreds of thousands of words he's written. He doesn't remember the day we decided to live together or our wedding. Our first night together. Nothing. Two days ago, I fell asleep with the love of my life, the only person who knows me at the deepest core of my soul, and yesterday morning, I woke up again next to a stranger. Someone surprised to see me walk into our bedroom with coffee in my hand, something I've been doing every morning for pretty much the last twenty years. It's not easy."

59

"I understand your frustration, Ms. Lewis. I will try to shed some light on this matter and find a way to get your life back to normal. Can you tell me if your husband has ever suffered from severe migraines or epilepsy?"

Patty replied without thinking too much. "No, never. Perhaps some light headaches when he writes for too long into the night, or when he drinks a few too many glasses. It happens occasionally."

The doctor nodded. Rivers of ink filled her notebook pages.

"Do you remember if your husband had any heavy physical exertion in the previous days? Any stress or something that worried him a lot?"

This time, Patty shifted her gaze from her hands to the window and took a few seconds to think. "Not that I remember. It's been just like any other day. It didn't seem like he had anything to worry about. He didn't look stressed. The night before we enjoyed watching TV. He usually goes to the gym, without being really committed to it. He's a writer. He's quite lazy when it comes to body training and physical strain." Patty offered a hint of a tender smile.

"Does your husband use drugs or medication of any kind?"

"No. A long time ago we smoked marijuana together. Just a few times. As for prescription drugs, Robert doesn't like to use them, even when in need. He takes a pain reliever every now and then. Maybe when he drinks too much."

"Does he usually drink a lot?" she asked.

"We have a couple of glasses of wine in the evening, while we watch TV. Sometimes we down the whole bottle and may have a little more. But I wouldn't consider him an excessive drinker. He's not a big fan of hard liquors, and on weekends, or on very hot days, he enjoys a beer at lunch."

There was a moment of silence.

"What do you think happened to my husband, Doctor?" Patty asked.

Foster sat back in the armchair and let out a long sigh. "It is possible that your husband is suffering from retrograde amnesia. What we need to figure out is whether we are dealing with a temporary or permanent memory loss. In both cases, this pathology can be triggered by a variety of causes. Sometimes, the brain temporarily erases memories as a form of self-defense. In such a case, it is rarely a permanent condition. It depends on the patient. In your husband's case, it looks like his brain decided to erase the last twenty years of his life, perhaps because of some childhood or adolescent trauma that was recently brought back to his memory. Therapy could help a lot, in addition to what you are already doing, which is to continue your life and daily routine normally."

"How long do you think this could last?"

"Hard to say. As I told you, and I want to be honest, there is a chance, albeit remote, that this amnesia will be permanent. But I don't want to scare you. I'm confident that your husband's condition is not that bad, and that everything will soon be back to the way it used to be."

Hearing those words, Patty lowered her gaze to her hands again. Her vision blurred as tears filled her eyes. She missed her husband, and yet he was waiting for her in the other room.

## VII

Robert and Patty didn't talk for most of the way home, each lost in their thoughts of how to fix this situation. As Patty remembered it, they had never faced anything as serious as this—no relationship crisis nor serious illness. Their lives had been stable, mostly free of tension and stress.

"I'm thinking," said Robert, breaking the silence "about getting together with the guys at The Cliff for a drink again tonight. Maybe seeing them more often, talking to them, or going to the usual places might help."

"That's a good idea," Patty agreed absently, still lost in her thoughts.

Robert turned his eyes on her. "Patty, can I ask you something?"

"Sure, but for the record, I'm your *mosquito*. You *never* call me by my name."

"Why on earth would I call you *mosquito*?" Robert asked, his expression amused but dumbfounded.

"In the early days of our relationship, when you were super focused on writing and studying at your desk, I would come from behind and buzz in your ear as if I were a mosquito." They both burst out laughing, and Patty added, "You know, just to get your attention."

"I actually remember that," Robert said and excitedly added, "That's one memory that's come back. But . . . wait. I came up with that nickname for you during our freshman year." He sounded disappointed.

Suddenly moved by that memory, one that they could actually share, Patty felt her eyes burning. It occurred to her then how important even minor details of their lives were. Now that everything seemed to have been erased from Robert's mind, she looked back with nostalgia. Perhaps, despite all the love they felt for each other, they had taken a lot for granted. Their love was not just another relationship, but a gift that they should have looked after as if it were a precious gem. She wiped the tear from her cheek and looked over at him. "So, what did you want to ask me?"

He took a deep breath and asked tentatively, "What was the worst time, in your opinion, during our relationship?"

Patty hesitated a few moments. Nothing bad had ever happened between the two of them. "I think it was when we moved to New York," she said finally. "You were not working, your book was not getting pick up, and it was hard for me, you know . . . between home and college, to take care of everything. You were frustrated, you felt like a loser, and the tension was high. But once you got over it, when you finally found your way, everything took a turn for the better. All the sacrifices and difficulties we went through made it more precious." As Patty spoke, her words filled her with pride and an awareness of just how fortunate they were.

Once inside the house, Robert looked for his cell phone, which he hadn't touched since the previous morning. He found it and stood staring at it. When Patty noticed, he explained, "I can't even remember my password. How am I supposed to call the guys?"

Patty smiled. "Your password is one-one-one-one. You never liked being complicated. You're terrible at technology. You'd rather write on the old typewriter your grandfather gave you."

Robert offered her a smile as he unlocked the device, which he had no trouble using. At least that was familiar. He hadn't forgotten the mechanics of things. "I'm going to ask the guys if they want to get a pre-dinner drink this evening. I hope they don't think it's too strange for me to be reaching out again so soon."

"It was your idea to keep your get-togethers to once a week. If it were up to them, you'd all be at The Cliff every night. But you wanted to keep it to just Saturdays so that we had six evenings together. I've always loved you for preferring to spend time with me." Having said that, she embraced him and held him tight against her body. She didn't want to let him go, ever.

***

The four friends sat at the same table as the night before. On Sundays, The Cliff was less crowded than usual. Robert chose a simple appetizer so that he could get home early and still have dinner with Patty.

"So, Rob, any updates on your, ah, condition?" David asked.

"I met with a therapist today," he replied. "Apparently, I'm suffering from retrograde amnesia. The causes are still unclear though."

David frowned. "Is there any treatment?"

"Some therapy and going on living my daily life," Robert said with a shrug. "Science hasn't made sufficient progress in recent years when it comes to mental illnesses. It's scary. But, trust me, stress is the last thing I need right now. I have to remain calm and slowly try to get everything back to normal. After today's visit, I feel confident. Even if it is not something that happens all the time, it seems that in most cases one can completely regain their memory."

"What a strange thing the human mind is," John commented, taking a long sip from his bottle of beer.

Robert chuckled. "I can assure you of that firsthand. With your help and with Patty's, I'm sure I'll manage to get back to my old self."

Amidst all the "We're here for you, buddy" sentiments, Robert excused himself. As he headed for the bathroom past the bar, he noticed that the older gentleman from the evening before was sitting in the very same seat, following Robert with his eyes. The man's interest in him was making him increasingly uncomfortable.

Robert locked himself in the bathroom and stared at himself in the mirror for a few seconds. He nervously rinsed his face with water and stared at himself again. Anxious and confused, he took a few deep breaths and tried to relax. That's when he noticed a small painting on the wall, depicting a group of houses perched on a coastline. It looked to be an Italian landscape. Somewhere in the Amalfi coast or maybe the Cinque Terre, he wasn't sure. And yet, even though he couldn't be sure whether he had ever been to Italy, he felt that place was familiar. This was something he and Patty hadn't talked about—all the places they had been around the world.

Once out of the bathroom, Robert decided to confront the eccentric man at the bar. He approached him from behind. "Have we met?" he asked nervously.

The man gasped and turned around. When he saw Robert, he smiled. "You don't know me, Mr. Lewis, I'm pretty sure about it. And it's not because of your failing memory, at least not in this case. We never had the occasion to meet before."

Robert's heart pounded. "How do you know about my . . . problem?" he asked, bewildered.

The man smiled again. "Let's say your friends aren't as silent as the grave, you know. Rumors are flying."

They both turned to look at the table where David and the others were drinking and laughing, carefree.

"No," the gentleman clarified. "I casually overheard two of them talking about your situation yesterday in the parking lot, before you got here. I was intrigued by it. That's all."

"I may have lost my memory," replied Robert backing away from him, "but I'm sure I'm not fond of people being too curious about my life."

"Have you been having the dreams?" the man called to his retreating back.

Robert paused for a moment, then decided to ignore the question and went back to the table. He immersed himself in his friends' stories about their innocent escapades over the years and how they'd each met their wives. Nothing sparked a memory, but Robert found his friends entertaining and considerate.

On the way home, he couldn't stop thinking of that unusual encounter. *Have you been having the dreams?* The question still echoed in his mind. How could the man have known he was having nightmares?

Perhaps the older gentleman was some retired doctor or something like a mentalist — one of those characters who can read other people's minds just by looking at their faces. Perhaps he was doing it to milk money out of the rich and naive people who crowded the West Coast, luring fragile clients into paying in exchange for advice or solutions. He knew of similar instances but couldn't recall when he'd gained such knowledge.

Just before he crossed the threshold of his house, he tried to put what had happened out of his mind and decided to say nothing to Patty. He didn't want to cause her more stress. He found her sitting on the couch, waiting for him.

"How was your time with the guys?" she asked with a bright smile, one of the few things about her that he managed not to forget, that very sweet smile that made him get over any bad thing.

"It was pleasant," he replied as he sat down next to her, placing his hand on her leg. "The guys have been great, and I like them. Now I understand why I chose them as friends. Unfortunately, nothing came up that jogged my memory, and believe me they tried, but I guess that's the way it is for now." He looked around the room, and his expression grew mischievous. "Anyway, my beloved mosquito, I don't like the bright yellow paint we chose for this room."

"I know," Patty chuckled. "We argued a lot before we decided. You wanted something different."

"Different like what?" he asked curiously.

"A warmer color, but I'm not going to tell you which," she laughed. "This is the only thing we fought about that I'd rather you didn't remember!"

Robert laughed again and then suddenly grew serious. "Everything will eventually go back to normal, but I must tell you something important first."

"What is it?" Patty asked, straightening up on the sofa.

Robert leaned in and took her hand. "I want you to know that, even without my memory, I still love you. If I don't regain my memory, I won't be scared. I fell in love with you again, without knowing who you were, the moment you walked into the room holding those two cups of coffee. And I'm sure I would fall in love with you tomorrow if I were to forget everything again."

Patty gaped at him and then pressed her face into his chest and began sobbing.

He pulled her close. He knew her hysterics were a mix of joy and terror. "I'm here for you, mosquito," he whispered as he held her close. "No matter what, we're lucky to be here together. *Nothing* can take that away from us. I promise."

Patty broke away from his embrace for a moment and stared into his eyes. "No matter what happens, I will be here, my love. Whatever happens, I will never stop loving you, and we will be together, forever."

Robert's eyes now filled with tears. Patty kissed him, then kissed him again. She brushed her lips against his tear-stained face over and over, stroking a comforting hand through his hair. Then she slid her other hand under his shirt and pressed it to his chest. The couple lay down on the couch as they awkwardly tried to undo their clothes.

"Tell me what you'd like me to do," he whispered.

"I don't need to tell you anything. I'm sure I'll love whatever you'll do."

As Robert began to kiss her nipples, Patty moaned softly and let him pull her to him passionately. They tumbled off the couch onto the carpeted floor. Seized by passion for each other, they became one. The sweetness in her eyes was gone, giving way to uncontrolled desire.

They made love eagerly. He found again the body he believed he had forgotten. Nothing was as before, but he saw by the ecstasy on her face that what his mind could not recall, his body remembered. Everything became eternal, with no past and no future.

At the peak of her pleasure, she clung to his shoulders. "I love you, Robert Lewis."

"I love you too, mosquito."

***

Robert was dreaming again, wandering in that place where one could get lost or come face to face with his own demons — his fears and uncertainties.

He stood naked in front of the woman with smudged lipstick he had dreamed of the night before. This time, she was laughing, standing nude in a room he did not recognize. They were not alone; other people, whose faces he did not know, surrounded them, staring and laughing at their naked bodies. Robert seemed to be the only one who wasn't enjoying the moment. Humiliated, he frantically searched for his clothes, desperate to cover himself, to hide and disappear. He diverted his eyes to the ceiling, hoping to escape the surreal scene, when he realized that he was now sitting in front of the young man, the same one he had seen crying in his last dream.

"What's your name?" Robert asked him.

The stranger smiled. "Why can't you remember my name?" The smile vanished, and sudden sadness entered the young man's his eyes. "I thought I was important to you!" His face now contorted in anger.

With bafflement, the only emotion Robert seemed to feel for the boy was love. That he couldn't remember who he was left him frustrated. He stared at the young man for a longer time, searching for anything that might help him remember. His blond hair, the small scar on his chin. His gaze. Nothing came to mind.

Robert gasped in his sleep. Still deeply asleep herself, Patty took his hand, and he suddenly relaxed.

The dream didn't stop, and Robert found himself in the traffic on the street again. His chest was bursting with searing pain. He struggled to reach the corner, the same one he had dreamed of the night before. The homeless man was still there. So were the cars and the traffic lights. He felt he had to cross and get to the other side of the street. He was in a rush, even if he didn't really know where he was going. He just knew that something important was waiting for him on the other side of the street. Something that, if left unresolved, would cause him much anguish.

He leaned back off the sidewalk. That nauseating smell was back. He had to do something, maybe cross. He was about to step down from the sidewalk when he noticed a familiar scent and a voice he knew well.

He opened his eyes and saw Patty looking at him. She was still lying in his arms, her bare skin resting on his. "Were you having another bad dream?" she asked sleepily.

Robert looked around to make sure he was still home. "Same dream, only this time more vivid. Even more confused."

Patty slid her arms around his waist and held him tight, her eyes already drifting closed. Robert watched her face until her breath shallowed in sleep, then closed his eyes, hoping the rest of his night would be peaceful.

VIII

Robert awoke, frantically scanning his memory for any closed gaps his sleep might suddenly have filled. Still nothing. He found Patty in the kitchen and announced he wanted to take a walk on the beach alone.

A long, private staircase led from the villa and down the cliff to the sand. Once on the beach, he took off his sandals and headed north along the shoreline. He encountered many runners along the way. Of those who nodded at him, he was curious to know how many really knew him or if they were just being polite.

In the last hours, he had begun to wonder again if his memory would ever return. He tried to imagine what it might be like to live the rest of his life like that. He even considered how it would feel to start over from scratch every morning. In that moment, he realized how precious memories were, every encounter with the people he loved as well as those who came and went. He wondered what life would be like without the chance to sit down at a table with friends and ask, "Remember the time we . . ." A simple question, perhaps even trivial, but the answer contained all the strength and value of a memory. He realized how the process of making memories out of things was the glue that held everything together. Love. Friendship. Knowledge. Wisdom.

Nothing had emerged in those last forty-eight hours to unlock his memory. He would continue therapy twice a week, as he and Patty had discussed. Dr. Foster had even

73

proposed one or more hypnosis sessions. Robert readily agreed—anything to wake up from this bizarre nightmare. In the midst of all these thoughts, the one of the old man sitting at the bar came back in his mind.

***

He had walked almost a mile, when in the distance he saw the blue umbrellas on the terrace of The Cliff, which perched on a hill overlooking the ocean. He suddenly had an idea. He reached the stairs leading to the restaurant, sat down on the first step, put on his sandals again, and began that little climb. By the time he reached the top, he was panting for breath.

The dining room was still empty, which made sense, given the early hour. Robert approached the bar, where a young bartender was arranging some bottles on the glass and mirrored shelving.

"Good morning," Robert greeted him.

The young bartender turned and smiled. "Good morning, Mr. Lewis."

Robert was surprised that the bartender had recognized him. The young man must have seen him frequently for years when Robert met up with his friends on Saturday nights. Or maybe he recognized him because of his reputation as a writer.

"Can I ask you a question?"

"Certainly, Mr. Lewis. What is it that you'd like to know?"

"The last couple of nights I was here, I've noticed an older gentleman sitting right here at the counter." He pointed to the stool the old man frequented. "Do you know him by any chance?"

The young man seemed to ponder the question, and the his face lit up as if he had just had a flash of inspiration. "Of course. Mr. Redcliffe. Jack Redcliffe."

Robert grinned in satisfaction. "Can you tell me who he is? I happened to talk to him, and he seemed, let's say, a little strange. What do you know about him?"

At Robert's words, the young man spread his arms wide, visibly struggling to restrain himself from laughing. "Let's see . . . he's a multimillionaire film producer. He says he's retired, but from what I've read, he's still got his hands full, and there are whispers that he's working at a big new project with George Lucas. He's a peculiar guy. Oh, and also, he's the owner of this place. He first rented it ten years ago, then bought it, for the main reason, according to what he says, that the name of the club rhymes with his surname. He has been coming by for dinner, or just a dirty martini, every evening since he moved to Laguna Beach . And, as far as I know, he's not married."

Robert nodded, pulled a fifty-dollar bill from his pocket, and placed it on the counter. "Let's keep this between us. It would be awkward if—"

"No need to tell, Mr. Lewis, and thank you for the tip," replied the young man, as he quickly slipped the bill into his shirt pocket.

Robert left the club and walked back to the beach. Turning in the direction of home, he decided to go back to

The Cliff that night, alone. He would sit at the bar and talk to the old man—to Jack Redcliffe. He had to figure out why Mr. Redcliffe had asked him that question: *Have you been having the dreams?*

*Yes*, he replied in this mind. He had dreamed about the same faces twice. The same unknown places. They had all gotten lost in memory. The woman, the young man, the bum on the street corner. The pain again. Being naked. The lipstick. The tears. He had had the same dreams for two nights in a row, albeit in different ways and contexts. He wondered how that man could know to even ask him about dreams. He would ask him directly that evening and maybe get some answers.

***

Once home, Robert found Patty in the kitchen. Pots and pans were strewn about the kitchen, and it smelled delicious.

"I'm making one of your favorite dishes," she exclaimed proudly, looking up from a saucepan.

"And what would that be, mosquito?" he asked, slipping his arms around her from behind.

"You love Italian food and all pasta dishes, particularly the carbonara, with a little twist on the original recipe. You want me to use ham rather than bacon. A true sacrilege for Roman people."

Robert frowned. "Did I ever explain why?"

"First, you don't like bacon," she supplied, "and second, you like it better when I make it a little lighter, by mixing it with parmigiano cheese instead of pecorino."

"So, you're basically telling me that I don't like the carbonara."

The couple looked at each other and burst out laughing.

"I'm going to The Cliff again tonight," he said when they'd composed themselves. "But this time, I want to go alone."

Patty turned to him with a puzzled expression. "Why so?" she asked, her voice trembling slightly.

Robert tried to come up with a simple but effective reason. He didn't want to worry her by telling the truth. In the end, Jack Redcliffe could be a dead end. "To relax in a place that I apparently know well, and where I seem to have had a good time. I'd like to have a drink peacefully and try to find the connection with it in my mind."

Patty lowered her eyes. "Whatever you think, my love," she said calmly. "Just drive carefully, will you? And take your cell phone with you this time. You normally take it with you everywhere. Call if you don't feel well or if you think you're lost."

Robert hugged her warmly. "Don't worry. Nothing's going to happen to me. I just want to be alone there for a while to think."

Patty gazed up at him, longing in her eyes, and he bent his head to give her a lingering kiss.

"Now move over or I will overcook the pasta," Patty teased.

***

At seven o'clock sharp, Robert parked in front of The Cliff. The evening was warm but pleasant. Most likely, by that time, Jack would be sitting at the bar sipping his usual dirty martini.

After a few minutes spent scanning the entrance of the bar from the driver's seat of his Range Rover, Robert decided to head in. He was nervous, restless, and tense. The moment felt like a scene from a thriller in which the detective is called upon to reconstruct the plot of some crime and investigate to get to the truth.

Once he got through the front door, he immediately identified Jack, sitting at the bar with his back to the door. Robert inhaled deeply and went to sit casually down on the empty stool next to him. Jack looked over and smiled.

"So, you finally decided you wanted to know," Jack drawled, fiddling with the skewer of olives in the glass in front of him.

Caught off guard, Robert gaped at him. At that point, there was no reason to lie anymore. It would make him feel more stupid than he already felt at that moment. "I just wanted to understand why you asked me that question last night," Robert said firmly. "That's all."

Jack lowered his head to the counter. He was no longer smiling. "Jack Redcliffe. Nice to meet you," he said, offering a hand. "I think I know what you're going through right now. You've lost your memory, right?"

"Yes," replied Robert softly, embarrassment tightening his chest.

"One particular day, did you wake up as if nothing had happened but in a place you didn't recognize?"

"Correct."

"You felt fine health wise," Jack went on, ticking off his points on his fingers. "There was nothing wrong with you except that you didn't remember anything, and, more than anything, you couldn't explain how you got here."

Robert's pulse raced. "Yes. But—"

Jack laid a silencing hand on Robert's. "Doctors can't find an explanation. They fumble around in the dark and stammer about how far behind science is in this area."

"Yes," Robert replied, bowing his head under the weight of his distress. "My therapist says it could easily be retrograde amnesia, and that with time, it is possible that everything will go back to normal."

Jack gave him a pleased smile, but Robert picked up a subtle sadness in his eyes. A bitterness lingering from times long past.

"How do you know all these things, Mr. Redcliffe?" asked Robert.

Jack slowly wet his lips in his dirty martini. "Because I went through the same experience you're going through now. And, please, call me Jack."

Robert looked at him with astonishment.

"One quiet and sunny morning," Jack went on, with the tone of a practiced narrator, "I woke up in a mansion in Beverly Hills. Suddenly, I was the man I had always dreamed of being in my youth, a successful movie producer. I had everything but the memory of how I ended up here. I could remember my childhood and the days when I used to make small films with an old super 8 camera in the woods with my friends. I remembered my girlfriend at the time, Maria Sanuti. I looked her up; she's married, has two children, and lives in Miami. I remembered my family, cousins, brothers and sisters. They didn't want to see me, but I didn't know why. I was rich, and I was everything I had ever wanted to be."

Robert listened intently with a mixture of curiosity and disbelief.

Jack's expression grew haunted. "Until, after a few days, those dreams started. They were mainly the same nightmares. Unpleasant, baffling, and always with the same people in them. There was always a crying woman I didn't know, or rather, did not recognize. I'll talk about that later. All the other characters—children, men, or women who appeared in my dreams—were all unfamiliar faces. Then I dreamed of a storm in the ocean. I still feel the terror when I see the weather turning bad, because I could never get over the fear I felt in that dream. I never go into the water anymore. Sometimes I walk along the shoreline and wonder what it feels like to swim. Many times, I put my feet in it, with the certainty that that would be the right time to try. But each time, I change my mind. Yet, of the few things that I remembered, the most vivid one was how viscerally I must have once loved the sea."

A chill spread throughout Robert's body. "You're telling me—"

"Yes. I *never* regained my memory. At least not what I believed should have been the exact memories."

Robert stared at Jack, anxiety twisting his gut. "What do you mean?"

Jack smiled. "That's the kicker. Let's go take a walk, and I will tell you." He brought the glass to his lips again.

Patty stood at the window, her gaze lost beyond the glass. She stared out at the point where the ocean met the beach and merged in a continuing embrace of waves and sand. Robert had gone to The Cliff alone, and she was worried.

She thought back to the words they had said to each other the night before. What Robert had told her. Even without his memory, he still loved her. But something was not quite right. Robert was different from the person he used to be. Sure, this could have to do with his memory loss. But simple things like the clothing he chose from his closet, the way he made love as if every part of her was new to him, and even his gestures had changed in a way that only a wife could see.

Patty was surprised to wonder if she liked this temporary, or perhaps permanent, new Robert. She loved him. She always had, immensely. But that doubt had been plaguing her mind for two days now. She felt deeply troubled, even though all her memories were still there. She could not even imagine how distressed Robert must be in this absurd situation. She wondered how she would feel living the rest of her life next to a man who had stopped being the person she used to know. Someone with his same face, his same smile, but different somehow on the inside.

Through the glass, she could see the people walking on the beach, the surfers catching a final few waves as the sun began to disappear behind the distant horizon. Those were the same images she and Robert had been savoring for years. Everything was boringly and wonderfully the same. That's the way they had chosen to live. A life with plenty of healthy boredom, playing it safe with their small habits, of which they never thought they would tire.

She thought about the last memory he recalled of them, back when they were students. He was convinced he had said goodbye to her at the airport before leaving alone for New York—something that never happened. It was a strange thing. A distorted memory. For a moment, Patty feared that Robert's memory of leaving her and moving to New York alone, in reality, was what his subconscious would have chosen—as if he had regretted his choice to stay with her. For a moment, she felt guilty and responsible for what was happening to her husband.

She soon banished that thought from her mind. It wasn't possible. Robert had become everything he had ever wanted to be. He was a successful writer, and all his books had turned out to be best sellers. She recalled how happy and proud he was of his success, how thrilled he was when someone stopped him for an autograph on the street or when he was honored with some literary award. She still recalled how moved he was to see the first movie, based on one of his novels, on the big screen.

Robert had achieved every goal he had set for himself in life.

The only thing missing was the presence of a child. So many times, she had noticed the sadness in her husband's eyes when their friends would show up with their children at their home. She couldn't avoid seeing how tender he was when he took the time to play or surprise them with some magic game or spoil them with treats or snacks.

She knew Robert would have been a good father, but fate had decided on something else for the two of them. Again, she felt a little responsible even though they both knew it wasn't either of their faults.

Patty moved away from the window. She'd find something to occupy her time and mind until Robert returned. She thought briefly of her paint set stored in a closet in the guest room but chose a book from the bookshelf instead.

## IX

Robert and Jack left The Cliff and walked down to the beach. The sun was setting, and the sky had become red like fire. The surfers were slowly making their way back to their cars, with their boards under their arm.

*A typical, everyday picture of California,* thought Robert.

He had plunged into despair, reeling from all the terrifying things a near-total stranger had revealed. Apparently, Jack had never regained his memory, despite undergoing therapy and all sorts of tests. It was as if he'd had to start all over again, or rather from a random point in the life he used to have. He had to retrace his history, using information he could find about himself, in order to find who he had been until then.

Robert thought about how much harder it must have been for Jack, who didn't even have a wife to cling to for comfort and help, no one who could support him or guide him. He inevitably thought about how terrible it would be to suffer the same fate.

"So, what did you mean by 'that's the kicker'?" Robert asked as the pair strolled side by side, eyes on the horizon, leaving footprints on the shoreline behind them.

Jack Redcliffe inhaled deeply, seeming to scan the reddening sky for the right words. Robert imagined this would be neither easy to explain or make believable, and he knew it was going to be even harder to accept what he was about to hear.

"I started by piecing together whatever I could about the years of my mental void," Jack began. "Details mainly coming from newspaper clippings and a small notebook that I found in my desk drawer. I also had a few trusted friends I could ask questions. I spent endless weeks at home examining all the things that somehow I felt belonged to me. I tried to find out what my habits, vices, or desires were. Psychiatrists and psychologists were unable to give me answers. I was a man without a past. I went through endless therapies and hypnosis sessions. Nothing brought back a single memory to my mind. And to this day, I still don't have one. Except for my adolescence. Meanwhile I began to dream. I had terrible nightmares, every night the same ones."

"What kind of nightmares?" asked Robert, certain that he had found the connection between the two of them.

"I dreamed of a woman, a very beautiful one. I immediately sensed a strong attachment to her. A feeling that could be as strong as love. But she kept on crying and crying in front of me, and if I tried to comfort her, it would be in vain. It was like that every night. Then, there were other dreams. Like the stormy ocean, as I told you before, black skies and giant waves hurling incessantly against a lighthouse. Every night I went through the terror of that vision without understanding why I was dreaming about it. Every night, before falling asleep, I prayed that, for at least one night, I might be spared from that unceasing torture."

"When did you stop having them?" asked Robert looking down on the sand.

"After almost an endless year," replied Jack with palpable sadness. "As if nothing had happened, one night I fell asleep and didn't have any more nightmares."

In the long silence that followed, Robert processed what he'd learned. The silence separated what Robert now knew from the incredible truth yet to be revealed.

"How do you explain all that, Jack? What did you mean before, when you spoke of a memory not your own?"

Jack paused again, then heaved a sigh. "First of all, over the years, I attempted to study everything available to understand the possible causes of retrograde amnesia, whether temporary or permanent. I attended many conferences and met doctors and patients of all ages and from all around the world. I explored all kinds of therapy, both conventional and unconventional treatments. I even went to Brazil to see a shaman once, but all I brought home was malaria. I met with psychics and fortune-tellers of all kinds. Still nothing. One day, however, I decided to meet with people from my childhood, at least the few I remembered, including Maria Sanuti, who had been my girlfriend last I remembered."

"What happened?" asked Robert with growing dismay.

"When I saw Maria, I recognized in her the woman who had been appearing in my dreams every night for a year. Her hair was a different color, and she'd grown quite plump, which is why I hadn't realized it was her. There was no doubt I'd been seeing Maria in my nightly visions. The crazy thing is, Maria told me we had gotten engaged, but we ended our relationship after a few years for petty reasons. I didn't recall any of that."

"Incredible!" exclaimed Robert.

"Yes, it is. Before I sought her out, I remembered Maria as a young woman. In my dreams, she was older, the way she looked in real life. Maria assured me that we never spoke again after we broke off our engagement. Though it hurt, she said she had put me firmly in her past and that she was happy with her life choices. It was thanks to this discovery that I realized that, if I really wanted to get to the truth, I would have to look for it in a different way."

***

Patty sat on the couch with a glass of wine in her hand. Robert had not been in touch since he had left three hours earlier. She was still contemplating the strangeness of the situation and the contradictions in Robert's memories. Her husband remembered leaving her after college to move to New York. He remembered a flight he took, never to return.

Patty had a sudden flash of inspiration. She left her wine glass on the coffee table and hurried upstairs to the attic. She opened the door to a dimly lit room full of boxes. Late evening light entered through a small window in the alcove. She turned on the string lamp hanging from the ceiling and studied the various labels on each box — Christmas decorations, old books, stereo speakers, and so on. She moved one dusty box at a time until she found the one she was looking for: Robert - college.

She opened it. The box was filled with old photos from their college days, plus a few books, some notebooks, and a jumble of letters and papers. She frantically scattered everything on the floor until she found one small item. A plane ticket to New York from San Diego that had never been used. It was dated June 16, 1995, after his graduation ceremony, a few days before he'd moved into her parent's house with her.

Robert had been one step away from leaving everything behind, including city and college. She was the reason he had decided, at the last moment, to give up that plan. That ticket proved that his choice had been more than just a thought. He had felt a strong determination to take a step he never took. She had never seen before how close Robert had come to that life change. A wave of sadness overcame her. On the one hand, she was sure he had done the right thing by staying in San Diego with her, but on the other, she considered that he may have given up promising choices in his career because of his love for her.

As she sat in the corner of the attic, staring at the plane ticket in her hands, Patty wondered if that contradictory memory was actually the lost trauma from the past that was causing Robert's amnesia. Maybe something that happened days earlier had triggered that memory. Robert's regret was so strong that he had been left with a distorted impression of his past. She found it hard to believe that he'd regretted his choices. Robert's career had been brilliant. His lifelong dream of becoming a writer had come true in the best way possible. She was aware that it all was way too complicated and improbable, but it could be the answer to his dilemma.

Patty left the attic, taking the ticket with her. She would talk to Robert about it and see if her crazy theory could help him find himself. Holding that ticket and looking at it might create an emotion strong enough to bring back his memory.

Jack stopped walking and gave Robert a serious look. "What I'm going to tell you may shock you. It may seem incredible and crazy to you, a figment of a sick imagination. But I can assure you that in a way, it all makes sense, at least in my case."

"You're scaring me, Jack," said Robert, who was feeling increasingly unmoored with every passing moment since he had set foot in The Cliff.

"Don't be afraid. After so many years of searching, it was a revelation for me, too. Sad, but at least something I can live with. Something that gave meaning to everything and soothed me. But it's also something that, at first, I struggled against. If I had found out about it sooner, I might have been able to flip and rewind. And that's why when I learned of your recent condition, I tried to get your attention and talk to you about it. By finding out the truth, perhaps you could still make up your mind."

"Make up my mind?" he intoned, gaping at Jack. "I don't understand . . ."

"I'll start from the beginning, so that I can try to make it as clear as possible. After seeing Maria again after all those years and realizing that she was the woman in my nightmares, I began investigating the paranormal world. I read about people claiming the existence of a temporal and dimensional leap, something that has been theorized by many — the famous wormhole, the Einstein-Rosen bridge, Tesla's studies on teleportation and the quantum leap, just to mention a few. They are all intuitions, studies, and calculations that no one could ever really prove. We don't have concrete evidence that could prove the existence of other dimensions in the universe. We can't track down the effects or the cause of anything like that."

"What the hell are you talking about?" Robert stopped walking. "Are you telling me that you believe there are dimensions and that a person who is in one dimension can jump and find himself in another? Just like that, and for no reason?"

Robert started to seriously doubt Jack's mental health. In his youth, he had heard and read about such wild theories. He always thought they were the product of the imagination of crackpots.

As if picking up Robert's thoughts, Jack grabbed him by the arms and glared straight into his eyes. " I know what you're thinking right now. But I assure you that it is all true. I've spent years trying to put everything together and to understand what the heck happened to me. I compared my situation to those of others. Some were more confusing; others were just like mine — until I got to the most important point."

"And what would that be, Jack?" Robert demanded impatiently.

"The common denominator that unites all these experiences: a desire, a dream that was never realized, something you regret."

This seemed to ring true, and it piqued Robert's curiosity. "Can you explain it better?"

"There was one thing that connected all the cases I've studied, including mine, and it was the dream we had when we were young. Whether it is financial success or a loved one or an ambition. At some point, in our lives, we desire something so intensely that—here is the kicker—it comes true."

Robert nearly screamed in exasperation. "Are you implying that the life I am in right now was only the one I wished for, while I was leading another one? That one day I woke up in my *dreamy one* with no memory of my reality up until then? Without knowing how and why?"

Jack nodded. "The one thing that I couldn't explain for a long time is how it happened, how this sort of transition took place."

"Something tells me you've figured that out," Robert replied with a hint of sarcasm.

"Yes!" said Jack decisively, taking his empty gaze off Robert and turning it down the beach. "I discovered something very interesting during my research. I traveled a lot and got to know people with minds convinced of the most amazing ideas—all people who, one fine day, like me had awakened with no memory, in a life where all of them had nothing to regret, or rather almost nothing, but we'll get to that later."

As he spoke, Jack's excitement visibly grew. "All the people I met," Jack went on, "said that they were finally doing the jobs they always wanted or living in the place and loving the person they had been longing for since they were young. How did they know if that was what they had been longing for, if they lost their memory?" A spark of mischief entered Jack's expression. "Because it was the last memory they had. In my case, it was a passion for movies. The guy I met in Texas a decade ago? He'd always wanted to become an oil tycoon. And Tommaso, the barber at Piazza di Spagna in Rome, all he wanted was to meet the love of his life. Everybody's last memory was of the thing they most wanted in the world."

"Sounds like too simple an explanation, Jack. According to your theory, everyone who wishes for something hard enough could actually turn it into reality."

The old guy smiled, as if he had expected such a reaction. "You're right, it does sound too simple. But there are other determining factors in this sort of dimensional shift. And you won't like all of them, once you hear what they are."

Robert kicked a shell at his feet, sending it tumbling toward the waves. "Honestly, I'm not liking anything you've been telling me," he said with mounting despair. But his interest had been growing by the minute. He didn't want to accept what Jack was telling him, but he felt desperate for something—anything—that could explain what he was going through. That desperation made him consider believing Jack's bizarre story.

"In the beginning, I couldn't believe it myself, and I wondered the same things you are now. How could this be true? How does it happen? Why? And more importantly, why me? But the more people in my same situation I interviewed, the more I became aware of new details. Long story short, one day we all woke up with no memory of years and years of our lives. We were all suffering from permanent retrograde amnesia. We are all intelligent people, Robert. I'm not talking about some crazy visionaries I met on the corner of Times Square or in a mental hospital. We all remember vividly everything that happened from the moment we got out of our beds with our blackout. Since that day, I've never had any new memory issues. The same thing happened to them."

Robert opened his mouth to speak, but Jack raised a placating hand. "It sounds crazy and twisted, I know. Anyway, we were all carrying a little memento of a past quite far from the time of our blurred memory. We could recall our adolescence, our youth, even our early childhood, but we had memory gaps spanning years, even decades. We all found ourselves resurfaced in a life we had dreamed for in our youth, which we could recognize because it played some role in our last memory before the gap. However, we all began to have nightmares and visions, some of us just for a few days, others for weeks. For me, it lasted for an endless year. In every story I heard, there was a common element—our dreams kept repeating themselves, night after night, re-dreaming the faces and places we had dreamed the night before. Only a few of us were able to understand what those dreams meant.

"In my case, I could identify Maria only after seeing her in person, although not right away. That's because in my dreams, she was not the girl I remembered. Now, don't forget what I'm saying. In my dreams, I was seeing her the way she looks *now*, even though I had not seen her for more than two decades, and we both agreed on that. How was it possible that I could dream of Maria the way she looked now rather than how I remembered her?"

"Maybe, for some psychological reason, that's what you wanted to believe," Robert suggested.

"Come on, Robert!" Jack insisted. "I dreamed of that face for more than three hundred nights! That's not random! Point is, the story is not over yet."

Robert would have liked to act skeptical, but he couldn't. "I hope so, Jack. Because you're getting me more and more confused here."

"That's where a gentleman named Justin York came into the picture."

**X**

Patty poured herself another glass of wine and perched herself back on the couch. It was getting late, and she still had no news from Robert. Worried, she grabbed her cell phone and decided to call him.

"Hello!" he answered after a few rings.

"Where are you, my love?"

Robert hesitated a few seconds before answering. "Hi, Patty, I am sorry, but I lost track of time. I met this guy, and we are walking on the beach. I'll explain when I get home."

Patty rotated the stem of her glass nervously between her fingers. "Okay. Sorry, I didn't mean to check up on you, but I was worried. I'm glad you found someone to talk to. I'll be waiting for you."

"Okay. See you later."

"Later? Wait, Robert?" she called out before he hung up.

"Yes?

"I love you," she said without hesitation.

"I love you, too," he responded quickly.

She let the cell phone drop on the couch and went back to her glass of wine. Robert's voice had sounded strange to her—too calm and controlled. She wasn't feeling better after that call; on the contrary, it left her more confused about her husband's state of mind than before.

***

Jack gave Robert a hard stare. "Don't even think about telling your wife about this. She wouldn't understand. I imagine she's experiencing almost as much confusion as you are right now. It would only upset her. She wouldn't believe you, and you'd scare the hell out of her. And you would risk losing her. For sure, she would start doubting your mental health. This experience is difficult to understand even for those who directly experience it. Imagine for those who haven't."

"I don't even know what to think about all this," Robert replied. "I can't imagine that Patty could. Chances are she will have me locked up in a mental hospital."

"Trust me, you'll understand," Jack said softly. "You'll understand *everything*."

Robert diverted his gaze to the beach. He was still in disbelief. In the last two days, the life he had lived — and couldn't remember — had been turned upside down. In that moment, standing in the light of a lifeguard tower lantern, he felt as if he had stumbled into a paranormal story of which he was the protagonist. "Who is Justin York?" he asked after a few moments of silence.

Jack turned toward the dark expanse of the ocean, from which came only the steady sound of waves crashing against each other and on nearby rocks. "I met Justin York after a few years of researching these bizarre theories. He is a big shot at some New York bank, or rather he used to be. More recently, he has been giving conferences all around the globe as a life coach. He travels from city to city giving speeches on the importance of dreams, life goals, that no one should ever stop dreaming and all should pursue their goals with determination to do everything they must to achieve them, living life without the regret of not having tried or having given up. The pivotal point in his teachings is that dreams do not just magically come true. They must be achieved instead. Now, I know the words I'm about to tell you will disappoint you one more time. If your dreams are suddenly fulfilled as if by magic, something you really care about in your life will disappear in that moment."

"What exactly do you mean by that?" Robert asked, dazed.

"First of all, according to Justin York, dreams actually can come true by . . . let's call it magic. Even if I wouldn't really call it that, because it's not about magic. But, in that specific moment, for that dream to come true, you will lose the most important thing in your life. A positive thing or person that you used to have, without knowing how important that thing or person was for you."

"Okay, you're talking about a guru, going around the world making easy money by creating illusions," Robert joked. "Though I can't remember, I'm sure it's not the first time I've heard that story."

Jack displayed a mischievous smile. "I was thinking the same way, when I read about his meetings and even when I went to listen to him at one of his speeches in Chicago."

"And?" Robert pressed.

"And nothing. I decided to meet him in person. I paid a fortune for that. So many people were looking to meet him face to face. To be able to talk to him in private didn't come cheap. But, as I told you before, since my dream was to become a successful film producer and I had already woken up with more money that I could spend, I paid what there was to pay. I showed up at the door of the hotel suite in Washington D.C. where York was staying during his lecture tour."

"What did he tell you that was so important for my — I mean, our case?" asked Robert nervously. "What else is there that I should know?"

"Everything there's to know."

***

Patty walked over to the window and peered out at the now darkened beach. She couldn't stop thinking about Robert's words. He said he had met someone. Was it a man? Maybe a woman? Whoever it was, they had been walking in darkness or in the dim light of some streetlight. She wondered what they were talking about. The silence rang with deafening doubts.

Robert's actions had become almost predictable over the years, not because he behaved in a predictable or trivial way but because she knew him so well that she could sense his every emotion. As much as Robert loved being in the company of his friends, he had always been shy and wary of strangers. To be considered a friend by him was not an easy thing to do. He was very introverted and cautious around people he didn't know. She wondered if Robert had changed in this respect as well. Once more, she asked herself how much she liked this other new aspect of the man she had married.

It was getting very late. She had always had faith in her husband. After all, he was a methodical creature of habit. It was a particularly delicate moment. Patty had seen how fragile Robert had become. Even though she was trying not to overreact, she knew it was more than normal to be very concerned for him; so far, there was no apparent reason for his memory loss. What if it were to happen again? What if in this moment, while in the company of this unknown man or woman, he lost his memory again?

She tried to remain calm, but her mind filled with distressing thoughts that would give her no respite. She didn't intend to call him again. During the earlier call, though his voice had sounded strange and unusually low, she felt there was nothing alarming.

She poured herself another glass of wine and turned on the TV to distract herself. But the fast images and slow words running on the screen could not fill the emptiness she felt inside.

***

"Everything? What else is there?" asked Robert, quivering.

"Everything related to how the leap happens. What causes it and why it happens. Is it because of some specific event or a desire or a thought? All about the *thing* that can cause in an instant what Justin York calls the *leap*."

"And how does Justin York know this?" Robert blurted.

"Because Justin York not only took the leap. He did it again—he jumped back."

Long seconds of deep silence followed. Jack looked deeply into Robert's eyes, as if he could see into his soul. But Robert was becoming increasingly distraught and tired, and his thoughts had sunk into a macabre emptiness. The old man's hand trembled as he held it in an awkward position, before reaching toward Robert's face. Everything had become unfamiliar and surreal, starting from the gloomy shadow that descended from the lamppost onto his cheeks to the familiar smell of the sea.

"He jumped back?" Robert asked incredulously, breaking the silence.

He'd startled Jack with his outburst. The man took a second to compose himself and explained, "Like us, Justin York woke up one day with no story on a yacht in the Caribbean Sea. His life was that of a man who had won the lottery and spent his time traveling. Besides owning the boat, he was always in the company of beautiful women and indulged in drugs and other vices. At first, like you, and like me, he didn't realize why. He initially blamed it on the abuse of substances and addiction. This was also the opinion of the doctors. Unlike us, York didn't make a big deal out of it. He was a superficial man. He had awakened to a fantastic life, one that anyone would dream of. As with us, the only thing that bothered him was the unpleasant and never-ending series of dreams, or rather nightmares.

"In his macabre visions, he constantly saw a man, a handsome young man crying desperately in front of him. York felt for him a deep, unresolved affection that was almost love. The more he saw the young man suffering in the rooms of his sleeping mind, the more he felt the need to console and pity him. Each time he tried to reach out to him, but he failed. He would have liked to hug him, but the dream was constantly changing. He saw the same man, albeit in different contexts, night after night. For example, in a big city or some fine restaurant crowded with people who were enjoying themselves. In all those scenes, the young man would not stop crying.      As the days passed, York began to look forward to the nightmare in which he could see him again. Despite all the pain, sorrow, and grief he saw in the man, York couldn't help but miss him once he was awake. Soon he began to think obsessively about how to get in touch with him even during the day but without knowing where to start."

Jack waved his hands absently. "Weeks and months passed. Justin plunged into a delirious abuse of drugs and alcohol. The women who kept him company no longer gave him any satisfaction. Nothing was like it used to be before the amnesia. Or, at least, it was no longer the same life he had been told about after he lost his memory."

"Did Justin York tell you what his last memory was?"

"Yes. He was in an office in the Lehman Brothers building. He had just started working there and was thrilled. He remembered the satisfaction, after spending so much time studying, of being hired by a big Wall Street firm."

"What happened next? You mentioned a reverse jump," asked Robert. Anticipation and a fascination with the topics of their long conversation were finally growing in him.

"Yes, Justin made it back, but clearly not on purpose. Other situations happened that involved different desires, and he suddenly found himself thrown back into his previous life — the one here."

"Previous life? Can you elaborate?"

"You still don't get it, Robert?" Jack demanded, raising his voice. "Before losing our memory, we were in another dimension. Another life, with another job and possibly another woman."

Robert staggered back, shaking his head. He didn't want to believe it. Jack's words were an overbearing force entering his most intimate space. "What happened to Justin York?" he asked, almost in a whisper.

"After a night of partying, under the influence of drugs and alcohol, Justin found himself on the deck of his yacht. Around him there was only darkness. He was too high and, as he was trying to make his way to his cabin, he slipped and fell into the water. The girls and crewmen on the boat were sound asleep. He presumably drowned."

"I don't understand," Robert stuttered in puzzlement.

"The instant he touched the icy water, he panicked and thought of the young man crying in his dreams. The confused state he was in, because of his excesses that night, prevented him from reacting and swimming. Within minutes, without realizing where he was, he lost consciousness and let go."

"I don't understand. Do you mean Justin York died only to awaken in another life?"

"No, he went back to the same life he had left a few weeks earlier. He awoke in a hospital bed where he had been lying in a coma since the morning he had attempted suicide. His memory was unaffected. On September 15, 2008, the day

Lehman Brothers declared bankruptcy, Justin York lost everything he had: his job, his savings, and his self-respect. He locked himself in the bathroom of his luxury apartment and cursed the world and all those years of studying and working late into the evening. He grabbed a bottle of the tranquilizers he used to take in times of great stress and emptied it, standing over the sink. Before he swallowed all of them, his last thoughts went to the huge fortune that had vanished just in one day."

"Let me get this right!" interrupted Robert, irritated and incredulous. "In 2008 Justin York attempted suicide, but he didn't die. He instead went into a coma and wound up in a hospital bed. In that instant, he woke up with no memory in a completely different life. He found himself to be a millionaire with a yacht who traveled the world. One evening, confused and wasted out of his mind on drugs and alcohol, he fell into the water and drowned. In that precise moment, he woke up in a hospital bed as the Wall Street financier who had attempted suicide?"

"That's right. And guess who was sitting at his bedside?"

Robert looked out over the night-dark ocean, out where there was no more horizon, no more noise, and total blackness. He stepped toward the ocean with hesitation as he whispered the answer, "The young man who was always in his dreams."

"That's right. His boyfriend. When he opened his eyes, he found himself face to face with his lover in tears. Although the young man looked distraught, lonely, and tired, he had never left York's bedside. In his selfishness,

Justin York, after losing all his money earned over years of working so hard, had decided to end it all. He was unable to accept how much he had lost, his shattered dream of power. He hadn't thought about his boyfriend, his love, the suffering he would cause to the people who loved him. He didn't think about his man."

Anguished, Robert couldn't believe the surreal, impossible story. How could he be living in a parallel reality? He didn't have time to ponder it further as Jack went on. "When I met Justin York, through all my research, I could finally connect the dots. The solution I had persistently sought for years became suddenly clear. Justin York had lived in a time space that was not this one, but rather another dimension. It happened when he attempted suicide. The night he fell into the water and nearly drowned, he was shot back to his prior life."

"But how could such a thing happen? Why him? Why us?"

"According to York, the whole thing happens the moment life is about to leave us. If, in that moment, we're holding on to unrealized dreams, the spirit, or what you might call the soul, refuses to give up on life and indulges, if I may use that term, in our ultimate desire. That's how the soul moves into another dimension."

"It *creates* another dimension?" asked Robert, his eyes widening in confusion.

Jack shook his head. "There are probably infinite dimensions occurring at the same time, by a number of elements we are not aware of, or that we just don't yet understand. We don't *create* it. We *leap* to it."

"That's absurd," whispered Robert, lowering his gaze to the wet, compacted gray sand beneath his feet.

"As I already told you, when Justin York awoke from his coma, his memories were intact, including the ones he experienced in the other dimension."

"Couldn't it have been just one of those dreams people have during a coma?" argued Robert.

Jack smiled as if he had expected that question. "It would mean that, right now, you and I are in our dreams, since we haven't woken up on the other side yet. Do you think you're just in a dream?"

Robert shook his head. He couldn't disagree with him. He was feeling very much alive. Still, he felt the need to fill his lungs with the ocean breeze, just to make it clear to himself.

"It's not totally wrong, though, to consider it a dream," Jack continued.

"What do you mean?"

"I mean that the whole thing happens because of an unfulfilled dream. According to York, like I said before, people tend to live on dreams without doing the work to make them come true, without pursuing them. And when it all goes dark, for some, the dream comes true. But at a high price."

"What price?"

With a distressed look, Jack lowered his head and put his hands in his pockets. "As I mentioned before, the price of leaving the most important things behind. In Justin York's case, it was his beloved partner. He had dreamed of wealth, and the moment he lost it, instead of looking at what was most important in his life, he decided to commit suicide. In his mind, there was only the thought of all the material fortune he didn't want to give up."

Assuming this crazy theory was true, Robert could not help but wonder about everything he had left behind in the previous dimension, a past that was now unreachable for him. He also wondered how big his dream might have been that he would give up all his past to be there.

"Jack!" Robert exclaimed with a wince.

"Yes?"

"Do you think right now I'm dead or in some coma in another dimension?"

Jack sighed. "Here is the big news. According to Justin York's conclusions, as long as we are having nightmares, it means we are alive in the other dimension. Those nightmares are peeks into the other side for a few moments. Our mind is still alive in the other dimension and interfering in some way with this dimension. When the nightmares stop, it means that life on the other side has left us and we stay forever in this second dimension, without memory, until the end of our days, to rebuild a new life in the time and space in which we are physically present. With our dreams fulfilled, but without that which we have lost forever." As he spoke, Jack's enthusiasm seemed to leave him, replaced by bitterness at the sad truth of his lost life.

"Jack, you stopped having nightmares after a year. You don't have those dreams anymore. Does it mean that—?"

"That I died," the old man interrupted, his voice broken with anguish at the truth, "most likely, a year after the leap."

Robert shuddered and turned away to sit on a nearby rock. Everything became even darker in his mind. He felt close to fainting, his mind spinning in terrified shock. Try as he might to deny Jack's crazy theory, somehow it all made sense.

## XI

By the time Robert crossed the threshold, it was past midnight. Patty had dozed off on the sofa, still clutching the half-empty wine glass.

Robert stood in front of her, watching her tenderly for some minutes. He wondered what unfulfilled dream he could have had. What was his last wish before he took the leap? Was it fame and wealth? Or was it her?

As he stood there, gazing at the woman for whom he felt immense love, he spied a plane ticket lying on the coffee table in front of her. Confused, he picked it up and saw it was the ticket his father had given him more then twenty years earlier—the same ticket that, in his few remaining memories, he had used to leave San Diego.

That must have been the moment it all happened, the split second that created the leap and made it possible for his two dimensions to meet—the moment his father had handed him that ticket. The leap wasn't about success or money. It didn't happen because of a material desire. It had to have been about her.

Maybe in an unhappy moment of his life, close to his near death, Robert had wished to have her back. In an instant, he thought longingly of Patty and regretted leaving her.

Patty moved between the sofa pillows, and her eyes opened a crack. When she saw Robert standing in front of her, she winced and sat up. "You had me worried sick!" she said, getting up and hugging him, sleepy and clearly dizzy.

She must have done a lot of drinking while she had waited for him. "Where have you been all this time? I was so worried."

Robert pondered in silence for a few seconds. What was there to say? He had just discovered that the best explanation for his loss of memory was that he was in another dimension—a dimension where his dream and ultimate desire to be with her was true.

Jack had advised Robert not to reveal this crazy theory, this pseudo-reality, to his wife. She would never believe him. And the obligatory course of treatment would surely involve analysis sessions with a shrink, a probable regimen of antidepressants, or even his admission in some psychiatric hospital. It wouldn't be easy to convince anyone else to believe this story. How could he explain anything like that? He couldn't believe it, either.

He decided to tell Patty the most plausible thing he could come up with. "I met an old psychiatrist," he said in his shaking voice, hoping she would believe him. "Someone who has been studying amnesia cases for years."

In hearing those words, Patty slipped out of his arms and looked at him with surprise. "And what did he tell you?" She didn't waste time.

"He told me about other cases like mine. The studies there have been made on those who have lost their memory, his personal research __"

"And? Did he tell you anything useful?"

Robert clammed up for a few more seconds, studying Patty's distressed expression. "No, mosquito. Nothing very useful at all."

That day, Susan arrived early at the intensive care floor of Lenox Hill Hospital on 77th Street. It was a wet and rainy morning. As she had been doing every morning for the last three days, she carried her thermos of coffee and a book. She headed toward the room occupied by her husband, where she would sit at the foot of the bed until lunch, at which point she would eat something at the hospital café before going back to sit in the room, where she would stay until sunset.

She had decided to take a break from work. How could she possibly focus on her job and her patients as if it were a day like any other? Brian, on the other hand, would drop by for a couple of hours in the afternoon before going back to the university campus, where he would try to study and try not to think too much.

Susan's grief for Robert's condition consumed her. After hours of staring at his helpless body lying in front of her, she would end the day on the sofa at home, where she would fall asleep until the next morning.

As she entered the room, she saw Dr. Crown, the surgeon who had operated on her husband urgently three days earlier. "Good morning, Doctor."

Dr. Crown turned and stared at her with glassy eyes. "Good morning, Dr. Lewis."

"Any news?" she asked as she put her coffee and book down on the small table next to Robert's bed.

The doctor lowered his eyes to the medical chart in his hand. "I'm afraid it's not good. As I told you after surgery, your husband is in a stage-three coma and is being kept alive by the pulmonary ventilator. Today, however, we believe he has progressed to a stage-four coma."

"What does that mean?" she asked in a trembling voice.

Dr. Crown took a deep breath before answering. "It means he has gone from a deep coma to an irreversible one."

"Irreversible?" stammered Susan.

"I'm sorry, Dr. Lewis. We will complete the final stimulation tests, before declaring him brain-dead. I am afraid there is little hope, given the latest results. Really sorry . . ." He concluded by placing a hand on her shoulder.

Suddenly without strength, Susan let herself fall back in the chair.

Robert would never wake up again. The man who had stood by her side for two decades was leaving her forever. Emptiness yawned inside her and a shiver rattled her spine, as if her own soul was also leaving her at that moment. She couldn't hold back the tears. As she brought her hands to her wet and desperate face, she felt an excruciating pain in her chest.

"I'll leave you alone with your husband for a bit," Dr. Crown said quietly. "I'll be back in a little while to discuss what to do."

Susan dropped her hands abruptly, exposing a face she was sure was contorted with pain. "What exactly do you mean?" Susan demanded, rising to her feet.

The doctor sighed again. "When we declare him brain-dead, you will have to decide if you want to continue to leave your husband attached to the machine or not. If it is as we think, then there is no hope of revival, and keeping him in this vegetative state will not bring him back. But that will be your decision to make."

Susan's heart sank. Nothing would bring Robert back to her—nothing. Now the question was, how long was she willing to keep hoping for a miracle?


Robert fell into a deep sleep next to Patty. They lay next to each other, holding hands in the darkness of their bedroom. It wasn't long before he was pulled into one of his nightmares.

This nightmare was new. Robert stood again in front of the woman he had dreamed of before. This time, she was taunting him cruelly, and he felt anger and resentment toward her.

Then everything went dark. He turned around and saw the young man, standing beside him with tears in his eyes. All three of them—the woman, the young man, and Robert—stood on a lawn. The young man was talking to him, but Robert could not hear his words. Everything was happening in total silence. Darkness fell again.

The honk of a car horn shattered the silence. Robert turned and tossed in bed. He was on the street again, in a state of confusion. The same voices, screams, and even smells. This time the homeless man greeted him, showing his mocking toothless smile.

Robert stared at him in disgust. The bum stopped waving and gestured for Robert to come closer, then stretched his arm out to him. At the sight of the man's worn, wet hand, Robert grimaced and tried to step back. But he was frozen like a statue.

His body turned in bed again. He was now lying motionless on a bed he hadn't seen before, staring at the white ceiling. A drop of water fell from a small crack above and hit him in the middle of his forehead. Another one followed. And another once again, without interruption. He twisted his head around and saw that the room was full of water, high enough almost to swallow the bed.

Sweating and panicked, he opened his eyes. He looked over in the dimness of the room and saw Patty. This time, she had not woken up. He looked up at the ceiling. He could hear the constant crashing of the waves outside. He thought back to old Jack's words. He thought of Justin York, the leap, and the dream.

*Dreams don't magically come true*, York had told the old man.

He wondered again about the price he had had to pay. What or who had he left behind?

If he had jumped almost to his death, thinking about Patty, it meant he was living alone or with someone less important to him. Who were the people who were crowding his nightmares? Who was the woman for whom, in his dream, he almost felt hatred? And the young man who wept next to him? The homeless man? What was the meaning of everything he had experienced in those brief images?

Robert lay in bed with his eyes open the rest of the night until the sun began to shine. The strong light filtering through the curtains diffused itself all around the room and shone upon Patty. She was still sleeping peacefully on her back next to him. Her face seemed relaxed. The more he observed her, the more certain he was of how much he loved her. With or without memory, this woman was everything to him. Whatever he had left behind in the other reality, another dimension, could not be worth more than her.

He didn't care if, like Jack Redcliffe, he had to live the rest of his life remembering nothing until that fateful morning. He would build new memories with Patty, beautiful memories and a carefree life. In time, he would get used to it and live a normal life, like everyone else did. In the end, he wasn't the only one. As Jack had told him, there were others around the world who were experiencing the same situation. Other people who, like him, had taken the leap. He would adjust as others had. The way Jack had done.

***

After breakfast with Patty on the terrace, Robert got up from the table and rested the dishes in the sink. She approached him and hugged him from behind.

"You're so quiet today, my love. Are you alright?"

Robert turned to face her. "Everything's fine. I'm still thinking back to last night, but all good."

"You have an appointment with Dr. Foster today. Don't forget that. It's important."

"I won't. As you know, I have a mind like a steel trap in these days."

The two shared a laugh and embraced each other.

But Robert's laugh was fake. He was frustrated, and he knew that he wasn't going to meet Dr. Foster that day. He would look for Jack again. He still had a lot to ask him. His head was full of questions and things he would need to understand. During his sleepless night, he had also made the decision to meet with Justin York. The old man's words were not enough for him. He couldn't just trust what Jack had told him about York. He needed to hear it firsthand.

While Patty was in the shower, Robert sat down at his laptop. He typed Justin York's name into Google and immediately clicked into his website. The home page was advertising his tour around the world. A different city every day. Robert thought about how exhausting it must be for him to perform incessantly, traveling from one city to another. Getting up on a stage and doing the same monologue every time, keeping the same enthusiasm and fortitude. Staying strong and charismatic every time. It had to be exhausting. To last that long over the years, Justin York had to really believe in what he was doing.

Robert consulted York's conference calendar and noted that the next day he would be in Phoenix and the day after that in San Francisco. He figured he shouldn't waste such a great opportunity — that is, if Justin agreed to see him privately on such short notice. But maybe Jack could help him with that.

As Robert carefully studied the website, looking at video clips and photos, Patty surprised him from behind. Robert almost jumped out of his chair.

"How come you're interested in Justin York?" she asked, patting her hair with a towel. "Did any memory come back to you?"

"Sorry, you caught me by surprise. Do you know Justin York?" he asked, eyes wide with wariness.

"Yes, of course. You know him, too! We went to one of his lectures two years ago in Los Angeles."

Surprised, Robert stood up from his chair. "Did we really?" he almost shouted.

"Yes, my love. He's a life coach, someone who talks about life and dreams. About never giving up. He talks about meditation, the butterfly effect, and the fact that life is not as simple as it appears to us. In fact, it is shaped and intertwined with the lives of others, according to the choices we make. Even the smallest decision can change both our fate and that of others. It was an interesting experience, I have to say."

"How did we end up going there?" Robert pushed.

"It was your idea. You came home one day and suggested that we should go. You had already bought the tickets. But why are we talking about this now? Really, did something come back to you?" She took his hand and squeezed it with palpable trepidation.

Robert remained in thoughtful silence for a few moments, trying to reflect on and metabolize the news. There had to be an explanation for this absurd coincidence. "I'm not sure. Let's talk about it later," he mumbled as he headed for the bathroom. "I'd better get ready for my appointment with Dr. Foster."

## XII

Jack was sitting at the bar, enjoying the view and the cooler weather. The temperature was perfect, and one could be easily pampered by the light breeze that came up from the ocean to the top of the cliff, on which The Cliff stood.

When Robert entered the club, Jack immediately raised an arm to draw his attention. The billionaire made him take a seat in front of him and asked the waiter to bring Robert a cold beer.

"Did you have another nightmare last night?" he asked as he nosed the aroma of the Pinot Grigio that had just been poured into his glass. "I save the martinis for the evening," he added as if it were an important fact.

"Yes. More than one, and like the others. Different in details, but always with the same people and the same feelings. The same fears."

Jack sighed. "It means you're still alive somewhere else."

Robert leaned in. "I still have a thousand questions, but I need to tell you something important."

"Go ahead," replied Jack. He took a sip of wine.

"This morning, I went on Justin York's website. I was thinking of having a meeting with him. Patty surprised me while I was doing so and asked me why I was looking into that. She was wondering if I started remembering something since, two years ago, I had arranged for us to attend one of his conferences in Los Angeles. Don't you think that's a bizarre coincidence?"

Jack sat pondering for a few seconds. "We'll ask him directly tomorrow morning."

"Tomorrow morning?" replied Robert with surprise.

"Yes. We have an appointment with him tomorrow at his hotel in Phoenix. I called him this morning and told him your story. He is eager to meet you."

"But . . . I must tell Patty!" stammered Robert. "I don't know how to do that. It's a six-hour drive."

"Who said we were going to drive? Tomorrow morning, at seven o'clock, we leave in my helicopter. We'll be there in a couple of hours."

Robert balked. "Helicopter? I don't think I like that idea."

"How do you know?" Jack teased him.

"I don't," he replied with a smirk.

"Well, you actually do know. And that's what I'd like to talk to you about today: emotions. But first, let's get back to you. You said you have a lot of questions. What are they?"

Robert tried to get his thoughts in order. He was still distracted by the fact that he would be meeting with Justin York the next morning, and that in order to do that, he had to take a helicopter. "First of all, I'd like to understand how you were able to rebuild your life. Is there something specific you hold on to?"

Jack took another sip. "First of all, as you know, I spent years trying to figure out what had happened to me. I didn't give up until I had it all clear in my mind. Only then I decided to enjoy what this life had given me. I didn't want to waste it, if you know what I mean."

Robert nodded. "Of course. But what changed when you stopped dreaming?"

"Not much. It was after I met Justin York that I began to understand what it really meant. The first night without dreams was a relief, though I never stopped wondering what those nightmares had meant and, for a few of them, I even got an idea. For others, I guess I will never know."

"What did you understand?"

"For a long year, I dreamed of two particular things. One was Maria. The other was the ocean. For the first one I still felt love and closeness. For the second, however, only terror and pain. I think Maria was the important thing that I gave up, while the ocean . . ." Jack stopped talking and diverted his gaze to the immense horizon before him.

"What about the ocean?" Robert asked.

"I believe that's what killed me."

***

Patty immersed herself in one of her scientific magazines to keep her mind occupied. Without something to take her mind off Robert and his bizarre memory loss, she would drive herself crazy. When she heard her cell phone ringing from the kitchen, she put down the magazine and ran to answer.

"Hello?"

"Hello, Mrs. Lewis?" asked a female voice.

"Speaking. Who is this?"

"I'm calling from Dr. Foster's office."

"Is something wrong?" Patty blurted. "Has something happened to Robert?"

"No, ma'am. It's just that Mr. Lewis didn't show up for his visit today, and the doctor was wondering why."

A few endless seconds passed before Patty could put her thoughts together. "Really? He didn't show up? I don't understand. He left this morning saying that he was going to do so. I don't know what to say. I'll call him on his cell phone right now and get back to you."

"Thank you, Mrs. Lewis. Let us know."

Patty hung up and, with trembling hands, punched in Robert's number. She couldn't fathom what was going on in her husband's mind. But something had definitely changed in him the day before. That morning, he had seemed disturbed and distracted. He had assured her that he would go to the appointment with Dr. Foster, but he hadn't. Why? This was the only question she could ask herself as she held the phone to her ear, waiting for Robert to answer. If he hadn't gone to see Dr. Foster, where could he be?

After a few rings, his voicemail picked up, and she started panicking.

To calm her troubled thoughts, she paced the room, trying to figure out what to do. The idea that something might have happened to him panicked her. She decided to drive to downtown Laguna in search of him. She pulled on a tracksuit and tennis shoes. Their 2000 Audi TT convertible was parked in the garage. It was Robert's old car, but they both used it very rarely. They preferred the comfort of the

Range Rover. Besides, she didn't like traveling with her hair in the wind.

Patty struggled to reverse out of the garage, uncomfortable operating the manual gear shift, and the car jerked a few times as she maneuvered out onto the street.

***

"What makes you think the ocean was the cause of your death?" asked Robert.

"If not that, then why would it constantly be in my dreams? That fear, the intense and exhausting suffering that I experienced each time I dreamed of it—I see no other reason. If it is true that the leap happens at a time when one's life hangs by a thread, I think that in my case it was something related to the sea. If it took me a year to die, there's a good chance that I slipped into a coma for causes that could be related to drowning or, maybe, an embolism during a scuba dive. I couldn't come up with another explanation, and, at this point, I would rather not have to wonder anymore."

"Sorry. I didn't mean to rip open your wound."

Jack leaned back with his elbows on the table. "It's not a problem. Your turn. Tell me about your nightmares." He stared Robert straight in the eye.

"I dream of a woman and a young man," he began. "I also dream of a homeless guy. He's always standing on the same street corner. The other night he even stretched out his hand to me. When I dream of the woman I feel anger, pain, and regret. The young man, on the other hand, is always crying. He's been sobbing like a child in all my dreams. He talks to me, but I can't hear what he is saying. We try to touch each other. We stretch out our hands, but nothing. I can't feel him. There's only silence. Whereas when I dream of standing on that street corner, noises get amplified around me and smells get stronger. You know, people's voices, horns honking. Even the sharp smell of exhaust from the cars."

As Robert spoke, Jack listened intently, as if he was trying to catch some clues that could help to identify the things Robert had left behind in his previous life, those good things that he had lost and failed to keep from his previous dimension. Any detail that might indicate that he too had been in a coma or something similar.

"Do you recognize the two people you see in your dreams?" asked Jack.

Robert frowned. "No."

"I think in order to reconstruct what you experienced, who you were, what kind of life you were leading before the leap, you're going to have to undergo what I call the emotional test."

"What is that?" asked Robert, intrigued.

"I have learned to understand something about my parallel life," said Jack, as he sought a more comfortable position in his chair, "by analyzing my emotions in this one when faced with situations. For example, I know I wasn't rich before or, at least, nowhere near as rich as I became when I woke up."

"How could you tell?" he asked, curious and captivated by the topic.

"Based on the fact that I was amazed and fascinated. Not only did everything seem new to me, but I felt I wasn't used to that standard of living. As if it were something that wasn't possible for me before. Now, I already told you about my fear of the ocean. Let me try to explain myself better. The ocean and its waves simply terrify me. Since the moment I woke up again, I have never stepped foot in the water even though, deep inside, I feel a close connection to it. And that's why I believe my death — *my leap* — had to do with the ocean. Finally, I think I'd been very much in love in my other life. I wasn't alone. I had a deep and intimate connection with someone, with Maria. Since I woke up, in all these years, I have not been able to fall in love with anyone. It's something that happens to a lot of people, I know. But I feel like it's different for me. I always feel a sense of guilt. It happens every time I wake up in the morning, in bed next to a woman. Every single time, either I feel empty or like I had just been cheating on someone. I hope you can understand what I'm saying." There was a hint of embarrassment on Jack's face.

Robert watched the old man, struggling to fully understand and imagine those descriptions applied to himself and his own life. He felt that he loved Patty deeply, a feeling he probably had even before the leap. In fact, he felt certain that she had been the motivation for his leap. But the catalyst for the leap — that near-death event Jack had insisted on — he hadn't yet figured out.

Jack interrupted his thoughts. "Now it's your turn to focus. Try to distinguish the emotions you've experienced in recent days when in certain situations or toward certain people."

Robert looked toward the thin line between the sky and the rippling ocean. "I feel a strong attraction for the ocean. It fascinates me, and I never get tired of looking at it. I am in love with its smell, the sound of the waves the moment they break. Perhaps, in my alternate life, I haven't had many opportunities to enjoy it. Then, I feel a great love for Patty. Something that, even if all this were true, exists beyond time and space. And that very feeling, the intensity of it, makes me strongly believe that being with her was my last wish before the leap."

"Anything else?" asked Jack.

Robert was silent for a few seconds. Yes, there was another strong emotion he'd been feeling.

"What else, Robert?" Jack urged.

Robert replied with deep and painful sadness, "One of the things I felt I was missing the most in my life, after waking up that first morning, was a child. It was such a strong feeling that I immediately asked Patty why we didn't have any."

Jack kept quiet for a little. Robert knew that, at that moment, the two of them were contemplating the same answer. But as he spoke this confession aloud, a clear likelihood arose in his mind. The young man in tears who appeared to him every night in his nightmares . . . Robert had finally identified the enormous price he'd had to pay for his dream to come true.

"Robert . . ."

"You don't need to say it, Jack," Robert whispered, his chest aching with grief. Jack's tentative tone told him the old man had arrived at the same conclusion. "The most important thing I left behind must be a son."

Jack winced sympathetically. "These are just conjectures. Perhaps we'll learn more tomorrow when we meet with Justin York."

Robert nodded and grabbed his pint of beer, looking unsuccessfully for relief from his anguish in the honey-colored drink.

***

When Patty arrived in front of The Cliff, she saw the Range Rover.

"What the hell are you doing here?" she whispered.

She parked on the side of the road and headed toward the restaurant. As she entered, she spied Robert in the distance. She recognized the man he was talking to: Jack Redcliffe, the famous film producer. It had never occurred to her that they might know each other. She stood for a few minutes in shock, watching them talking and pondering her next move. Then she turned and walked away.

She drove in the direction of their house, determined to ask Robert to explain later that evening when he came home. Knowing that he was hiding something from her made her feel sad, disappointed, and angry. She couldn't comprehend why he had not told her what was happening while she was desperately trying to help him get through this terrible experience.

As she sped home, for the first time since Robert had awoken without his memory, Patty felt utterly alone. It was almost as if he were abandoning her. She blinked back hot tears.

## XIII

When he returned, Robert found Patty sitting on the terrace, gazing at the horizon. She did not turn around as he approached.

"Something wrong?" he asked, stopping in front of her.

"Where have you been?" she asked without looking away from the view.

Robert fell silent. He guessed she had found out about him missing his therapy session that afternoon. He knew that would be the case but hadn't planned for it. "Patty —"

"Actually, don't tell me," she interrupted in a shaky voice. "I know where you've been. I saw you at The Cliff, in the company of that old playboy."

Robert lowered his gaze to the floor.

"You didn't show up for your session with the therapist." He could tell by the strain in her voice that she was struggling not to shout at him. "Tell me, what could be so much more important than that, at such a time? Was that the man you were with the other night? What are you hiding from me, Robert? Please tell me what's going on."

No matter how crazy it seemed and how difficult it might be to believe, Robert knew it was his duty to tell Patty the whole truth. He couldn't let her continue to stumble around in the dark. She was hurt, and his behavior was making it worse. He sat beside her and took a deep breath, groping for the right words to explain his incredible discovery.

"Mosquito, I will tell you," he said, his voice trembling, "even though you'll probably think I've gone crazy. I'm going through a phenomenon of sorts that I find hard to believe and understand. But if you listen to me and, above all, trust me, perhaps many doubts will be clarified."

Patty looked bewildered. "You can tell me anything, " she said, grasping his hand. "I will surely understand."

Robert seated himself on a deck chair, facing her. "It won't be easy for you to accept," he began and then told her about his conversations with Jack Redcliffe. He shared Jack's story, his research, and his findings. The connection between the nightmares and his memory loss. The leap. The parallel dimension. Finally, he told her about Justin York.

Patty listened in silence. Robert couldn't read her expression: terror, disbelief, confusion, interest—maybe all four. He explained every detail as clearly as he could anyway.

When he finished, Patty's eyes were glassy. She was on the brink of tears but visibly struggled to keep a straight face. "My love," she said finally, with a note of disbelief, "are you sure this isn't just the product of the imagination of a man who's been left confused by what has happened to him? You're so desperate to find out why you lost your memory that you're willing to believe even such a surreal theory?"

Robert sighed. He knew how hard the theory was to believe. "I understand your skepticism and disbelief, but if you think longer about it, the whole thing makes sense."

"Do you mean that in another life, on your deathbed, you wished so much to find me again that you were thrown into another dimension?" she asked, her voice broken by tears and confusion. "That I am only the consequence of a space-time glitch? That nothing is true? Is that what you are trying to tell me? Do you *really* believe that?"

"It's not like that," Robert insisted. "As I understand it, the universe is made up of various dimensions that intertwine and change based on external factors. My desire caused these dimensions to cross. Each dimension is real, but it keeps changing, without us noticing. There is no time and there is no space. Every dimension is connected and influences other ones. And that's why, for example, two years ago I felt compelled to attend one of the Justin York's conferences. Probably, my two dimensions met at a certain point. But I'll figure that out tomorrow."

"Why? What's happening tomorrow?" Patty asked with a hard tone.

"Tomorrow I'm meeting with Justin York privately."

Their mutual silence emphasized both of their concerns. For the first time since he had begun his story, Patty took her eyes off Robert and looked down to the floor.

"Tomorrow morning, Jack will take me by helicopter to Phoenix where Justin York is waiting to help me solve this dilemma," he concluded.

"Are you trying to tell me that right now, you are also living in another dimension, while I'm not? And, in that dimension, you actually took that flight, and lived a different life of which you don't remember the details?"

He scrunched his face apologetically. "That's what I think, yes," he said, hoping she would give this theory—and him—the benefit of the doubt.

"I don't understand, Robert. I really can't," she replied, her words chopped by anger. She buried her face in her hands, and her shoulders began to shake.

Robert hugged her tight. "You *must* trust me. Look, if our relationship is really that strong, and if in all these years I have shown you that I am a mentally stable person who doesn't act on impulse, then you have to trust me and let me look into it."

Patty's sobs gradually petered off, and she peeked through her fingers. "Okay. Talk to Justin York. Do what you need to do. But you *must* promise me that you won't miss any more therapy sessions."

Robert let out the breath he was holding. It seemed she had decided to give him the benefit of the doubt. He gave her a shaky smile and said, "I promise, mosquito!"

***

As the helicopter rose off the ground, piloted by someone Jack said he trusted with the truth, Robert gripped the arms of his seat tightly.

Jack grinned. "I guess you are not an airline pilot in your other life. Or maybe you were in a plane crash," the old billionaire exclaimed with amusement.

Robert could hear him quite well through the headsets they wore. He grimaced and gave Jack a tense smile, fighting off the terror and dizziness this high-altitude experience induced. During the flight, Robert told Jack what had happened with Patty the night before. He had told her about the nightmares, his doubts, and the questions he would ask Justin York. Jack didn't look happy about it but shrugged it off.

"Let me ask you a question," Jack said abruptly.

"Go ahead," Robert replied.

"If you could, would you like to make the leap back?"

Robert turned his eyes to the view outside the window, where the Arizona desert alternated with the rocky hills on the horizon. "I don't know, Jack. If I wanted to wake up next to Patty so badly, it means that in my other dimension, I wasn't very happy. But living the rest of my life with this mystery, and no memory of twenty years of my life, terrifies me. And, not to mention, what of that young man who may very well be my son?"

Jack nodded. Robert knew this was a feeling his friend understood intimately.

"Besides the theories based on my dreams, I don't know what else there might be," Robert went on, without taking his eyes off the spectacle of nature outside the helicopter. "And I don't know anything about my last twenty years on this side. It's crazy how I feel when I think about it."

"The risk that one could go crazy is real, especially when you know the truth," commented Jack. "All the people I have met who suffered from the same amnesia tried to live life normally but never stopped wondering what happened. Like us, they can't figure it out and continue to live with all the uncertainties and vagueness created by the situation. Some consider the leap to be an unfortunate event. Others felt that something strange was definitely lurking behind their amnesia, although they could not identify what. All of them, however, move on with their lives but keep on wondering," said Jack.

Robert wondered, for the umpteenth time, how it would feel to live the rest of his life like that. Would wondering about his old life but never seeing it again, never knowing anything of himself except what his dreams showed him, ever be enough? And would he be enough for the people he shared this new reality with, living the last half of his life with most of the first half missing?

***

Susan sat in the waiting room in the ICU, waiting for Brian to join her.

For several minutes, she had been staring at the empty gaze in the eyes of the white-haired woman sitting across the room. She could see the despair on her face as she sat still as a statue, her skin as pale as a corpse. That woman was there, surely, because she too had a loved one hospitalized in ICU.

She wondered what that woman was feeling. She wished she knew what other people in this situation were feeling. Robert had just been pronounced brain-dead a little earlier, and she was waiting for Brian so they could decide what to do. They could leave Robert hooked up to a machine every day, hoping for a miracle from some God she personally didn't believe in or to let him go. Pull the plug. Release his soul. Watch him turn cold and blue in a matter of minutes.

As she was having all these thoughts, Brian entered the room. She stood up and ran to him. Mother and son locked in a strong, wordless embrace. They remained motionless for a long time, clinging to each other through their tears.

"We have to be rational, Brian. We have to be strong," she whispered finally, trying to support her son, who in that moment she imagined was crushed by a pain greater than hers. "Your father taught you how to be a man. I'm sure he wouldn't want to see you this desperate right now. Everything he has given you will remain in you, wherever he goes. Let him keep on living inside of you and be strong, as he would be."

The young man nodded, but he could not stop crying. A short time later, when he finally did, they sat across from each other.

"Mom, what exactly did the doctors say?"

"Dr. Crown told me that your father has gone from a deep coma into an irreversible coma," Susan said, as she held her son's hands in hers. "They ran all the tests. Your father is no longer responding to simulations and has lost all brain function. He's . . . brain-dead."

"Are you saying there is no hope?" whispered Brian, staring at his mother's hands.

"That's what I'm saying, my love."

"So, what happens now?" he asked with quivering lips.

Susan took a deep breath before answering. "We must decide if and when to allow the doctors to remove him from life support. When we want to let go of him." She held her breath then, so as not to fuel that pain even more. It occurred to her that even the air hurts when you don't want to breathe.

Brian's eyes stared sightlessly; his voice had fallen silent. Susan could not read what he was feeling in that moment and wondered if he felt anything at all, if he had gone numb.

"I need some time, Mom," he said at last, desperately. "Let's take some time."

"Yes, my love. There's no rush." Susan caressed his face as if he were still a small child. "We don't need to decide right now. Let's just sleep on it. There's no rush. There's no rush."

***

The helicopter landed on the runway in the private area of Phoenix Sky Harbor International Airport. Waiting for them not far away was a black limousine that Jack had rented for the occasion.

"There's whiskey in the bar if you want to relax before you meet York," the old billionaire said as they unbuckled their seat belts.

Though he knew a shot of whiskey could calm his nerves, Robert replied, "No, thank you. I want to be lucid when I talk to him."

Jack raised his hands in surrender as he took his seat in the spacious car. "I, on the other hand, will have a sip. These days I'm living a film I've already seen, and it's bringing up old tension."

The ride to Justin York's hotel lasted fewer than twenty minutes. The men didn't speak. They were both deep in thought, wondering what would come out of this meeting and how the famous life coach would answer Robert's many questions.

Upon their arrival at the hotel, they were escorted by a young woman from Justin York's staff into a small room reserved for private meetings located behind the lobby bar.

Robert and Jack sat on the two closest chairs around the table, waiting for the guru to arrive.

"Mr. York will be here any minute," the staffer assured them, handing each man a bottle of water, which they accepted gratefully.

After a few minutes that felt like an eternity to Robert, the door opened again. Justin York made his entrance, followed by an assistant carrying a folder under his arm. Papers and pamphlets peeked out from the folder's open sides. The assistant placed the file on the table in front of his boss and quickly left the room.

Justin York was a man in his fifties. He was about six feet tall and wore his graying hair military short. He carried himself with the self-assured grace of a celebrity, his lean physique not quite hidden but not quite on display in a white sweatshirt over jeans and sneakers. His smile exuded charisma. "Good morning, gentlemen," he said with delight as he sat down on the opposite side of the table.

Jack and Robert returned the greeting, as York arranged the documents in several stacks on the table in silence. Then turning to the old millionaire, he crowed, "You're looking good, old man."

"Thanks, Justin. You don't look too bad yourself. I hear you're a world traveler of late, giving lectures all around the globe. Congratulations!"

The life coach offered a contented smile and spread his arms. "Yes, thank you. I haven't slept more than two nights in a row in the same bed for practically a year now. But I'm pleased. People are responding well."

His guests nodded.

York turned a serious gaze toward Robert. "So, Mr. Lewis, first of all, it's a pleasure to meet you. I've read some of your novels and found them very fascinating. Jack suggested to me that you may be one of those who have experienced what we call *the leap*."

"Well, yes, according to Jack. What I do know for sure is that I have lost all memory of the last twenty years of my life. I woke up five days ago in a bed that didn't feel like my own, next to a woman whom, in my few fuzzy memories, I recognized as my girlfriend from college. I hang out with friends I don't know, and I walk in a city whose streets I'm unfamiliar with. For the past four nights, haunting faces appear in my dreams. They give me a sense of anxiety and fear. And then I met Jack. He told me all about his life, and then revealed to me the existence of this leap theory. And here we are." Robert ended his brief speech feeling awkward.

"Did Jack tell you about my experience as well?" York asked.

"Yes, but I'd like to hear more from you. I'm here to figure out not only what happened, but also what will happen to me in the future."

York moved slowly in search of a more comfortable position on his small chair. Then he looked straight at Robert. "Years ago. I woke up in a place I didn't know. Suddenly, I had no past. Or at least, I was left with no memory from my adolescence until that moment. I remembered very little. I felt intensely uncomfortable. The only positives were that I had tens of millions of dollars in the bank, and I carelessly spent all my time on a luxurious yacht named *Cristina*, in the company of three beautiful female models. After doing some research, I discovered that I had won the lottery. I was sailing between Mexico, Florida, and the Caribbean. I had a house in Aruba and a garage full of sport cars.

"I believed what the doctors had told me. It was a strange form of amnesia. Perhaps it had been induced by my endless abuse of drugs and alcohol. It was still unclear whether it would be a temporary or permanent state. However, I let myself be carried away by that recklessness, as if that had always been my life and without making a big deal out of it. From what I could understand, I had no stable relationships with family members or with women. All my relationships were superficial."

York ran a hand over his silver-tinged hair. "I just kept on going, almost as if nothing had happened, except that I was always trying to remember. I kept trying to recover my memory. But nothing. Moreover, I was constantly plagued by nightmares. They soon became a steady phenomenon in my already chaotic and vicious existence. In the most recurrent dream, I saw a young man crying, heartbroken. Every night. Dream after dream, I began to look for a way to comfort him and to connect. Nothing. I always woke up the minute I was about to reach him with my hand or talk to him or something like that. I found myself hoping and waiting eagerly to see him again. It was like I had fallen in love. Like being in an unusual relationship.

"Until one night, I was drunk and high and fell into the sea. I still remember how dark and cold the water was. I couldn't tell which way led to the surface or to the bottom. I couldn't breathe, and my lungs took in water. I blacked out. The next thing I knew, I was gasping for air as I lay intubated in a hospital bed. In a life where I had been a rising star at Lehman Brothers. A few weeks earlier, I had attempted suicide by ingesting an entire bottle of pain killers. The young man in my dreams, it turns out, was my life partner."

"How can you be sure," Robert asked doubtfully, "that it wasn't just a dream you had while you were in a coma?"

York smiled, as if he were accustomed to the question. "After doing some research, I realized that what I believed to be just a dream was quite real. Even though I had never been to the Caribbean, I found the mansion in Aruba on the internet that I remembered from my dreams. My boat, *Cristina*, really existed and was for sale in the Port of Miami. But what really convinced me that this was not just a coma-induced dream experience was the fact that, during my coma, exactly three days before my awakening, a restaurant called Atardi reopened after renovation. The owners threw a party on the beach, which I happened to attend because, in my parallel life, I was a regular of the place."

Robert bit his lower lip. Even though he'd heard most of this from Jack, hearing it from York made him question how anything so unbelievable could be true.

"After I was discharged from the hospital, I continued my research almost obsessively. I devoted all my time to looking for similar cases. I finally met people who had gone through the same experience as me, Jack being one of them. By hearing their stories, the memories they were left with, the life they were living, and most of all the things they were missing, I realized there was a common element in all our stories: the sudden transition from one life to a completely different one, which I decided to call *the leap*.

"All the men and women I was getting to know had hit rock bottom at a particular time, when they felt haunted by regrets and frustrations. Each with their own desire and dream of having a different life. Each of us feeling regret for making poor choices in life. The disappointment at what they had managed to achieve and the unhappiness for how they were living. It so happened that during an accident, an illness, or, as in my case, an attempted suicide, they all expressed the ultimate desire to be somewhere else. To have the possibility to rewind their lives back to the moment when they made the wrong choice that led them to a dead end."

Robert and Jack listened to Justin York's words in profound silence. Robert hoped to hear something that could help him find some answers.

"All this gave me awareness that life is *not* a dream," continued York, "meaning that we can't live in regret and wait for someone or something else to magically change everything. There's no easy button that takes away the hard work needed to make our dreams to come true. It is never too late to take life into our own hands and go after that dream. To reach a goal that we thought was unattainable. There are two kinds of people, my dear Mr. Lewis, you say so yourself in one of your novels."

"What do you mean by that?" asked Robert, confused.

"In your novel *Love Has No Boundaries*, which you don't remember writing because *you* technically didn't actually write it, and I promise we'll get back to it in a moment, you stated that there are two kinds of people. There are those who are satisfied with what they have. They live happily and give value to what life has given them. Then, there are those who keep wishing for more. They are unfulfilled. They don't live. They survive, miserable, because they don't have what they wanted. I decided to become a life coach and dedicate my time to help this second group of people not give up—to stop waiting for something to magically happen in their life that will change it for the better. Instead, I would teach them to fight for their dreams. Fight to live a larger story without neglecting, in the meantime, the important things that are already in the one they are living. Because, my dear Mr. Lewis, in the moment we shifted between life and death, and we took the leap with our greatest wish clear in our minds, we all lost something else . . . something important. We may have left behind the biggest richness or the most important love we had in that parallel life, which, for some reason, we took entirely for granted. All three of us. You, Jack, and me."

Robert sat back in his chair, astounded. "How strange that this is in one of my novels. Here's something else that's strange. This morning, my wife told me we attended one of your lectures two years ago. Apparently, it was something I wanted to do. Just like that, for no specific reason. What do you make of that?"

Justin York smiled at Robert's question. "Fascinating. This is another theory of mine. I think our different dimensions intertwine at multiple points throughout our existence — or I should say our existences, to be correct. The dimension you're in now is the one you were longing for while you were living in the other one. I guess what happened was that in the most intense moments, the Robert Lewis on the other side would feel a . . . vibration, let's say, a space-time pull from this life."

Robert felt his head pounding, as if it could explode any minute. What Justin York was saying made sense on some very deep level, but he struggled to believe it and let go of himself in that truth.

"May I ask you," York interjected, "if you had one of those usual dreams also last night, Mr. Lewis?"

Robert nodded sadly. "Yes, I had the same nightmare, dreamed of the same people, though in different contexts."

"Fascinating," York said again. "You're the only one I've met while they're still having the nightmares, while they're still alive in the other dimension. We must hurry."

"What do you mean?" inquired Robert with curiosity. "Why *must* we hurry?"

"If we don't do something, you could risk being stuck in this dimension forever, like Jack did," said the life coach, gesturing to the old man in question.

Baffled, Robert looked from one man to the other. Until that moment, he had not seriously considered that possibility. Sure, Jack had brought it up in the helicopter, but he didn't think it was an actual option. No matter how confused and lost he was, the idea of leaving this life did not sound compelling—especially leaving Patty. If his desire for her had been what brought him here in the first place, she was probably absent in that other dimension.

"That's why you're here today, isn't it?" asked York, noticing Robert's confusion. "You want to get both your memory and your life back, am I wrong?"

"I came here to understand. I want to understand what's happening to me."

York rested his elbows on the table, clasped his hands, and leaned toward Robert. "As I told you, there are several dimensions. People live in several ones at once, only with different roles and different lives. They make different choices. They have different friends and partners. They reach different levels of wealth. Still, they are all aligned. Space and time do not exist in the dimensional realm. For those who experience them, each dimension represents the only life they have.

"You are in a particular situation. I will try to explain it to you in the simplest possible way. With your ultimate desire, when you were between life and death, you brought two of your dimensions together, made them overlap. Your soul, if we want to call it that, overlapped with your body—

the actual body you have in the other dimension. Both are true. I mean this dimension right now, here with me, and the one on the other side, where you are probably lying in a hospital bed, they are both real. If you don't try to put them back together, you could die on the other side today. You could lose your memory forever and, more importantly, you would remain misplaced in this life."

"Are you telling me that I have to *die* in this life to have a hope of waking up in the other one, like you did? But how can I know with certainty that I will wake up?"

Absolute silence settled in the room. York lowered his eyes to the table and took a deep breath. "It's one possibility," he whispered after a time.

"Right. But there's also another possibility that might give me more options. I stay here, I enjoy the life that this dimension has been giving me, next to the person I have probably always loved. The one I am loving now. I am wealthy and accomplished with my dream of becoming an acclaimed writer. While if I choose to take off from here, it will mean trying to return to a dimension that I don't remember and where, according to your theory, I was not happy. Actually, I was trying to run away from there. It would mean going back to something unknown, where nothing is certain because, in reality, on that side I could die moments before I manage to find the way to *leave* from here. What would happen in that case?"

"Then it would be over for you in both. That's true," York replied in a matter-of-fact tone bordering on cruel.

"I had a feeling you'd say that," exclaimed Robert, raising his hands in surrender. He let himself fall with his shoulders resting on the back of the small chair.

York sighed. "The young man who cries every night in your nightmares must be someone quite important to you. It seems he's missing you very much. For sure, you weren't happy. Maybe it's just something that happened in recent years. But, as I have told you, and as I have been repeating for years in my lectures, you can still change things there. If your ultimate desire was to continue living with the woman you wake up next to every morning in this life, then you could always decide in your other life to win her back or fight for her. At the same time, you won't have to give up that young man, probably a son, someone who has already suffered and will suffer again for your death in the other dimension." His gaze shifted to Jack and back again. "Jack told me that you and your wife don't have children, and it bothers you. Want to know why? Because deep inside, you've been feeling an emptiness since the moment you started living again. I realize that it may sound scary. It's surely a hard decision to make. You also don't have a lot of time to decide. But think about it. Think about it quickly and with everything I told you in mind. Because whatever your decision is, that will be your future forever."

"Or I may have no future at all," Robert interrupted impatiently. "Neither on this side nor the other one."

"True, the risk is a real one. Live here; die in the other. Perhaps die in both. But there is also a third possibility." With this, York got up from his chair for the first time since he had entered and began walking around the room with his head down, rubbing his hands together ponderously. "It's nothing sure, but according to my theories, my studies, and my analysis, there could be another way for you to get out from this situation." As he concluded, he stopped in front of the stained-glass window overlooking the street below.

At eleven o'clock that morning, Patty left Dr. Foster's office in a state of shock. She had gone to tell the doctor about the incredible theory her husband had meticulously laid out the night before.

She had promised him she would keep it a secret. She said she would trust him until his return from Phoenix. But after Robert had left the house that morning, she realized how absurd it all was. That crazy idea of his could only be the result of his illness. Maybe Jack Redcliffe was just an old man suffering from loneliness, who indulged Robert out of pity or some other senseless reason.

After listening carefully, Dr. Forster concluded that Robert was suffering from a mental disorder, one of the consequences of which was amnesia. She had considered this a worsening of his condition and suggested that he probably needed some pharmacological treatment in addition to therapy.

The doctor had also added that she had seen other cases of psychiatric pathologies, such as schizophrenia leading to memory loss. In many of these cases, the patient's condition had degenerated in such a quick and drastic way as to require hospitalization in a mental institution or the permanent use of high doses of anxiolytics and psychotropic drugs. Believing in paranormal realities, suffering from persecutory delusions, and constantly speculating on conspiracy theories and extraterrestrial invasions could also suggest this kind of disorder.

Patty had recognized many of those signs in Robert's behavior in the last few days. The more she thought about it and tried to put the pieces together, the more she felt her despair growing. She drove almost blindly, her vision blurred by her tears. From a carefree and comfortable life, full of love and complacency, she had fallen into a dark abyss filled with uncertainty, sadness, fear, and loneliness.

Robert was leaving her. His mind was already doing that, suddenly and without warning. Before that damned morning, five days earlier, he hadn't given any sign of what was going to happen. She felt like she might lose her mind, too. She almost wished that what Robert had told her was true, that there was no such thing as mental illness and that he really had woken up from another dimension. She sobbed even more at how insane that idea was.

She reached the house feeling like she was about to have a nervous breakdown and decided to fight that feeling by opening a bottle of sauvignon blanc. The bottle shook in her trembling hand. Seeing this, she burst into uncontrollable weeping and slid helplessly to the floor.

***

"What would this third way be, Mr. York?" asked Jack, who had remained silent until then.

York did not answer immediately. Robert presumed he was still thinking. The man looked out the window, as if hoping to find the right words to explain what was going on in his mind.

"Yes, Mr. York, tell us," Robert insisted. "What is this possible third way out?"

The life coach pivoted on his heels and placed his hands on the table, riveting his gaze on the two men. "Who can say for sure that that night, in my other dimension, I *died* by drowning? No one. I don't really know how things might have gone. All I know is that after I wished, in the grip of hallucinations, to meet that mysterious young man who appeared to me every night in my dreams, I woke up again in this dimension, in this life—my original one.

"Maybe everything went back to normal in the other dimension as if I had never made the leap in the first place. It is also possible that someone rescued the other version of me from the water, and now each dimension is now continuing its natural course. Just as I am talking to you right now, I may be still living in the dimension where I was a millionaire drug addict. Like I said, maybe someone witnessed my accident and resuscitated me after I lost consciousness. At that point, my two realities were no longer overlapping; they redivided."

Robert looked at him, dazed. "I know we've established that my body in the other dimension is probably dying. But are you telling me that my consciousness and the consciousness of the Robert of this dimension are merged? That I'm living, at least for now, in both dimensions?" he asked curiously.

"You always have," Justin replied with a shrug. "Until that moment when your two dimensions overlapped, you had been living the two different lives, oblivious of the other. I believe there is a possibility that once you reach the limit of life, as it happened for me, you can go back to your old reality and continue with your life, as I did. Perhaps you could improve it because of this experience with your new awareness, exactly as it happened for me. When you come close to death here, we could try to save your life so that you can also continue living in this dimension. We can't know whether you'd recover your memory here or if you would remember everything or nothing of this."

"You just said that you *believe* there's a possibility," Robert said as York reclaimed his seat, "and that we could *try* to save my life. Neither of these statements makes me comfortable. From what you're telling me, it's all just a hypothesis. A possibility. Forgive me, but I don't see it that way. For me, it is a huge risk either way. Let's say that, somehow, I am pushed to the edge of life in this dimension, and it's too late because I already died in the other one. In the meantime, in this one, I could not be saved. This means that it is over for me anyway, and in both realities. It makes the most sense for me to just stay here and live."

York sighed. "You are right, Mr. Lewis. I fully understand your puzzlement. Your fear. But these years have taught me something, one last thing I want to share with you before it is too late."

Robert waited with bated breath.

"If you remain here, you will eventually realize," York concluded somberly, "that you never *truly* lived in either of your dimensions."

***

150

Robert and Jack were speechless all the way to the heliport. Robert wasn't familiar with the fiery heat, the reddish desert earth, and that endless succession of warehouses and small buildings that crowded the landscape of Arizona. In the other dimension, he was sure he lived in a place that was less cramped and with a milder climate.

Robert wasn't angry at Justin York, much less at Jack. But he still felt angry inside. Angry for what had happened to him, for what the universe—or universes—had thrust upon him. He felt disappointed at the idea that, perhaps, he would live the rest of his life not being able to remember anything about his own past or that of another, a different existence into which he had been thrown by some universal force, a fate that was playing with his life, with Patty's life, and other people's lives—lives like that of the young man lost somewhere in space and time who, in that precise moment, was mourning him on his deathbed.

Justin York strongly believed that the best, almost obvious choice to make was to jump back, which meant attempting a sort of space-time travel that could only happen by reaching the edge of life and death, hoping to find himself alive on the other side but hoping at the same time to stay alive in *this* life.

Still, Robert knew that the life coach was right when he claimed that, had he done it differently, he would never have truly lived any of his lives. He wouldn't have remembered either of them. Perhaps he could have tried to rebuild a life from that point on, as Jack had done before him. But like that, it would have been just surviving, not living.

His only sense of certainty and source of strength, in that moment, was his love for Patty. That would remain with him. Nothing could take that away. If there was a risk of dying in either dimension anyway, here he would at least have her. As for the sad young man, from Robert's perspective, he was not living flesh and blood the way Patty was. He couldn't give her up for an apparition, could he?

Jack was silent beside him. Robert knew he was trying not to distract his new friend from his thoughts. There was only one place Robert could retreat to consider what to do, and that was within himself. Robert wondered what Jack would have done, given the opportunity to know all that Robert had gotten to know in time to change the course of this reality. If only he had found out before the end of those nightmares, when he was still alive in the other dimension, maybe, after all those years lived without any memory of his life, without the woman he felt he had left on the other side, Jack would have tried to jump.

But this was a choice Robert had to make on his own, even as time grew shorter and shorter.

***

As the helicopter lifted into the air, Robert turned to look at Jack.

"Jack, thank you for supporting me and helping me through this. I understand how painful it is for you to go through this again, after so many years. I also imagine you will be disappointed with my choice not to try to go back. I'd guess that if you were in my place, you wouldn't

152

hesitate. Maybe someday, I'll regret it. In the meantime, though, you won't be alone in your ordeal anymore. We'll stay friends who can commiserate with each other—and have some good times too, make new memories."

Jack smiled at him. "Thank you, young man. Thank you for your trust in me. Anyone else would have thought I was a scam artist. But you didn't. You're a very smart man. And you're wrong if you think that I am disappointed with you. I am not. To jump back is an arduous, courageous, and borderline insane choice. Something that cannot be made easily. As far as I know, no one has ever had to make a decision like this one. Not even Justin York. For him, it was a coincidence, a twist of fate. However plausible and probable it may seem that both lives could continue on, it remains only a hypothesis. And I know how much you love your wife. It's because of her that you almost certainly find yourself in this situation, so I understand your fears."

Robert listened carefully to Jack's words and noted his sincerity. He thought that Jack was right. There was so much at stake, and the possibility that everything could result in a double happy ending was based on an untried assumption. No, his fate had been written. He would live the rest of his life in a dimension he didn't know. The young man notwithstanding, he would never know what he had left on the other side. No therapy and no medication would bring back his memory of this lifetime—a memory, anyway, that didn't belong to him.
***

It was five o'clock when Patty poured what was left in her bottle into her glass. She drank it all in one gulp and slammed the empty glass on the table.

The room spun. Everything around her seemed to twirl in the air. She looked at her watch. She knew that Robert would be back any minute, and she didn't want him to see her in that state. She decided to pull herself together, get up, and take a shower, hoping she would feel better and shake herself out of the drunken daze.

Once in the bathroom, she took off her clothes and turned on the shower. Just as she stepped under the running water, she heard Robert walk through the front door. It occurred to her then that he would see the empty wine bottle on the coffee table, but she didn't care. She wondered if, amidst his own, he could feel her pain. Her discomfort. Her fear. *That* she cared about.

A few minutes later, she saw Robert's naked form through the foggy shower door. It brought a smile to her face and a yearning to her body. Oh, how she loved him. She opened the door and invited him to join her. They made love without speaking, without dwelling on their strange circumstances. They considered no yesterdays and no tomorrows. They loved each other with intensity. It was different this time—the way the new Robert knew how to do it.

They embraced each other under the stream of water. They kissed, felt one inside the other. They were one, enveloped in each other's pleasure, a pleasure that, for a few moments, managed to make the universe feel lighter, if only for a little while.

Once out of the shower, they slipped into their pajamas. Patty made a light fish dinner, and they sat beside each other at the table, barely mentioning the events of the day.

"How was the helicopter ride?" Patty asked, as if it were the only thing she was curious about regarding his trip.

"Scary at first," Robert replied, taking a bite of salmon. "But the vista below captivated me, and you know what? I almost liked it."

She smiled, but it faded quickly. "Did meeting Justin York help?" Patty asked, half fearing the answer.

Robert sighed and set his fork down. "I think so. Most of all, it helped me realize how much I love you. How important you are to me and how much our love has been the center of everything. And that is why I am *never* going to lose you. Whatever alternate dimension I left behind me, I'm here because I want to be with you."

Upon hearing those words, a chill ran down Patty's spine. She wanted to scream, "There is no alternate dimension!" but wouldn't, not in Robert's precarious state. Instead, tears of frustration spilled from her eyes. She realized how accurate Dr. Foster had been in her diagnosis and how much Robert's psychology had compromised his way of conceiving reality.

"Why are you crying, mosquito?" Robert asked.

Patty got up from the table and faced the glass window, turning her back to him. "I saw Dr. Foster today."

"You did?"

"I told her about your . . . idea," Patty went on, her voice broken with tears, "of parallel universes and space-time dimensions."

Robert snapped out of his chair. "Why? You promised me..."

Patty turned around, more tears spilling down her face. She hugged Robert tightly, but he didn't reciprocate, his arms dangling. "I know, my love, I know!" she cried pulling away and peering into his eyes. "But you need help. *You* need to trust *me* now. You're confused and lost. I'll do everything I can to help you get through this. You know I'm here for you. But let's give it a few more days, see if there's any improvement. Then promise me that if you're still feeling confused, you will go willingly for some more intense help."

***

Robert did not respond. She had not believed a single word the night before. She actually thought he was crazy. A sort of visionary madman. This new agony—her betrayal and her lack of trust—began to collapse the world around him.

His woman, the love of his life for whom he had traveled through time and space, didn't believe him. He knew what he was going through was hard to believe—even he found it inconceivable. It broke his heart to realize he had been naive to think that Patty would understand. Still, he understood where she was coming from.

He suddenly realized that his life here—everything aside from her—was unnatural. This wasn't a real life; it was forced by an error in the eternal flow of existence. It was a glitch, an anomalous occurrence of events. For the first time since awakening without his memory, Robert felt deeply alone.

# XV

In Robert's hospital room, Brian sat beside his mother in total silence, staring at the motionless body lying on the bed not far away. They were waiting for Dr. Crown to arrive.

Brian contemplated all the occasions when his father had helped him through tough times, spurring him on or supporting him, all the times his dad had smiled at him after one of his pranks. He could visualize the pride on Robert's face when Brian shared with him that he wanted to study law, like Robert had.

He thought back to all the times they watched soccer together, sitting side by side on the couch, the times they had cheered for some Italian or Brazilian team during international tournaments. He remembered the last few mundane words they had exchanged after that lunch on Lexington Avenue, before they parted ways, his father going back to his office and Brian returning to school. He knew he had told his father how much he loved him, many times. Still, he felt guilty for not having told him once more before they had gone their separate ways that day.

Tears blurred his vision. And yet, even as he looked at his father's almost lifeless body, he had the strange feeling that Robert was still there, as if a part of him had not given up. But he also knew that if his dad was still physically alive, it was only thanks to that machine, to the twisting tubes that held him prisoner in a world that was no longer his.

When Dr. Crown appeared at the door, Brian stood up and held out his hand.

"Good morning, Brian," Dr. Crown said with a shake. "Good morning, Dr. Lewis."

Mother and son nodded their greetings.

Dr. Crown was a tall, sturdy, and well-mannered man, his white hair suggesting decades in this profession. Brian briefly wondered how many times the doctor had been in this sad, awkward situation during his career.

"I am so sorry for what you have to go through," Dr. Crown said sincerely. "You will not be alone in this painful journey. The hospital therapist is available to guide you through this difficult time. Please do not hesitate to consult him if you feel the need."

"Thank you," Brian whispered.

The doctor lifted Robert's medical chart and scanned it before taking a seat. He heaved a sigh as mother and son sat in the chairs across from him.

"As I've explained, your husband and your father," he said, looking from Brian to Susan, "has gone from a stage of a third-degree coma, commonly called a deep coma, to a stage of fourth degree, better known as irreversible coma. That means that his body is essentially being kept alive by machines."

"I've read that some people have come out from irreversible comas," Brian interjected.

"I know," replied Dr. Crown in a calm voice.

Brian knew the doctor was trying to be as gentle as possible, but he felt rising anger.

The doctor went on, "I have read about those isolated cases, too. They are the result of errors made during stimulation tests. Many people call them miracles, but I can assure you that, in all my thirty years of career, I have never seen a patient wake up from the comatose state in which your father is lying now. I'm sorry, but I've witnessed no miracles during my career."

Brian wanted to hold out hope for a miracle, at least a little while longer, but the doctor made it impossible. Letting go of his mother's hand for the first time since they had taken a seat, he lashed out, "That's because you convince people to disconnect the machine before a miracle can happen."

Dr. Crown nodded. He did not seem offended by the outburst or the insinuation. "I understand your frustration, Brian. I also understand your wish to see your father wake up. But I assure you, if I had *any* hope that could happen, I would not hesitate to fight for it. Unfortunately, he is just not responding to any stimuli. We have done multiple tests several times. I would not be sitting here now if I did not know beyond a shadow of a doubt there's nothing that can be medically done to revive your father. You see his body breathing, and you believe that as long as he continues to breathe, there is hope. But what you are seeing is a sophisticated machine that manages to keep him alive but only physically; the brain is not functioning. The man you knew is gone."

The next moment was a yawning void. Empty voices, vacant air, blank thoughts. Brian looked at his mother. He could see her concern for his own mental state in her glassy eyes.

"Mom," stammered Brian as he stood up, "I guess the right thing to do is to let him go. I know that would be the first thing Dad would tell me if he could. I am sure of it. He would *hate* this."

The thought of his father muttering his displeasure brought a little smile to Brian's face. He then turned his gaze to the doctor, saw encouragement in his eyes to do the right thing. It would be selfish to leave his father in that state for who knew how long, and only on the off chance they might witness a miracle. They should let him go. "Doctor," he said at last, "tell us what we need to do."

Dr. Crown nodded and looked for approval in Susan's eyes. She nodded in turn.

"First," he said, "you'll need to sign some paperwork. We will do another round of stimulation testing for your peace of mind. That way you will be assured that you're not making a rash choice. By the day after tomorrow, we can disconnect the machine that's keeping Robert alive."

As Dr. Crown spoke, Brian walked over to the bed on which his father was lying helpless, took his hand, and squeezed it tightly in his own. He could feel the heat coming from Robert's skin, a warmth that would disappear in the next few days, when everything would become cold and lifeless. Robert's life would be over.

"How long will it be before my father dies, after we disconnect the machine?" he asked, his voice broken with pain.

"After we disconnect the ventilator and pull out the central venous catheter, your father's heart will stop after a few minutes," Dr. Crown replied. "Sometimes all it takes is just a few seconds. Other times, five or six minutes."

***

Exhausted after his confrontation with Patty, Robert fell asleep quickly. He found himself in a dark room; he could hear crying. Someone touched him. He felt the intense warmth of that hand grasping his own. It felt like a strong man's grip. Robert's mind went immediately to the young man he had seen every night, in every other dream, but he couldn't find him in the darkness.

A door appeared in front of him. He opened it.

He found himself on that corner again—among the cars honking, the shouting, and the same noxious smells. But unlike his other "visits" there, the homeless man was not in sight.

The traffic light was no longer green, and he couldn't cross. Cars whizzed past him. Suddenly, he saw the woman with the smudged lipstick on the opposite side of the street. He felt he had to catch up with her. He wanted to get a good look at her, to understand what she wanted from him. Why was she following him? He felt the discomfort of her pleading eyes on him, but he felt only animosity.

When he turned away from her, he was facing the young man; the background was hazy, but his face was kind, his features chiseled but gentle. With an outstretched hand, the young man invited him to follow. Robert reached for him and tried to speak but emitted no sound.

He gasped in bed. He plunged again into the dark, desperate crying ringing in his ears. That friendly hand caressing him.

He woke up to Patty peering at him in silence, waiting. "Another nightmare, my love?" she whispered.

He didn't reply and closed his eyes. He felt Patty's gaze linger on him awhile longer.

***

When Robert opened his eyes again, he was alone in bed. The sound of the running shower mingled with the roar of the waves and the calls of seagulls outside the window. He remained in bed, staring at the ceiling and thinking about the day before. About what had happened to Justin York and Jack Redcliffe. About what Patty had done. About the fact that she believed he was in need of psychiatric help.

He thought about the few memories he still had — the ones of him and Patty during college. Their love. His choice to leave San Diego for New York. That unused plane ticket, which had been sitting on the coffee table for two days now.

He thought about what kind of future he might have if he pretended he was having a nervous breakdown and had been delusional to believe in alternate dimensions. He would live out the rest of his life with Patty, secretly guarding the truth, a truth he would only speak about with Jack. He would wait for the nightmares to end — the sign that his life, in the other dimension, had ended. The moment of no return. In time, he would adjust to this situation.

He considered the handsome, vigorous young man who cried for him every night, the one he felt sure could be his son. Maybe, at that exact moment, in another facet of the universe, his body was lying on a hospital bed, comatose. Why? An accident? An illness? Or had it happened the same way as it had with Justin York, who had attempted suicide? These thoughts were still overlapping in his mind when Patty appeared at the door with a gentle smile.

Robert watched her as she dressed. He could see the sadness and disappointment in her eyes. His feelings for her ran deep, but now he detected an awkward sense of estrangement. He would never know or remember what they had experienced together during those missing years. He would never remember the first time they had made love as husband and wife, the excitement of it. He would never remember the disappointment of discovering that they couldn't get pregnant. He wouldn't have remembered any of that for the simple reason it hadn't been his life but someone else's.

He had stolen another man's life. In the most desperate moment of his life, he had wished to be someone else and live another reality. Another story. His wish had been fulfilled by a strange twist of fate. Now, here he was, in the body of another person who only looked like him, condemned to live forever in a lie. To be chummy with friends with whom he had never developed a relationship. To live in a house he had not chosen, with furniture he hadn't bought. To bask in the success of someone else's hard work.

Justin York's last words came back to him. He would never truly have lived. This life he had longed for would not truly be a life. Dreams don't magically come true.

He got out of bed and embraced Patty tenderly. He surrounded her with his warmth and held her close, quietly. She let him do it. Robert took a deep breath and steeled himself. In that moment, he knew the right thing to do.

"You're right," he whispered in her ear. "If I don't regain my memory soon, I'll take whatever steps the doctor deems necessary." He hoped this would buy him some more time, and the relief that crossed Patty's face suggested it would.

***

Sitting at Dr. Crown's desk, Susan finished reading and signing the pile of papers she had been given. It had taken almost an hour. Brian sat beside her in silence.

"Ms. Lewis, I will give all the documentation and the authorization to proceed to our legal department and the medical board. We will start once we are given the okay. It will take at least twenty-four hours. Most likely, we'll be able to unplug the machine by tomorrow night."

Susan and Brian nodded without speaking.

"Take as much time as you need to be with Robert. I've scheduled a session for both of you with the hospital psychologist tomorrow morning. I hope you will take advantage of it. I assure you that being able to externalize the emotions helps a lot during times like that. It's never easy to say goodbye to a loved one, and it's even less easy when the ultimate decision is up to the family."

Brian cleared his throat. "Thank you, Doctor. I'll meet with the psychologist. Thank you for your support during this incredibly difficult time."

Susan gave the doctor a tender smile. "Thank you, but I have my own therapist. And I'll try to spend the last hours with my husband. Thanks you for being here for us, Doctor."

They all got up together.

"I will let you know when it's time," Dr. Crown assured them. "I'm sorry I couldn't do more for Robert. For a doctor, every patient lost is a big loss."

## XVI

Soft sand sank under Robert's feet as he stood under the lifeguard tower near The Cliff at eleven o'clock in the morning. He had asked Jack to meet him there, but his friend had yet to arrive.

Just past the breakers, a group of surfers prepared to chase the waves that relentlessly crashed between them, before slowly subsiding to the shoreline.

The sky was clear. Not even a cloud interrupted the infinite blue stretching to the horizon. Robert closed his eyes and enjoyed the gentle breeze, the smell of the sea, the sound of the waves, and the seagulls crying. When he opened his eyes, he saw a man and a small boy building a sandcastle. The man went back and forth into the water with a bucket, which he first filled and emptied near the little one, who built small sand towers with the wet sand. Robert was close enough to hear the child's laughter. When a longer wave swept away the boy's work, the young father picked up the child and carried him to another spot on the beach, and then patiently resumed his comings and goings with the bucket.

From Robert's perspective, that was what a father's role should be: the constant rebuilding, patience, support, and tenacity in the face of negative events, showing his child the courage to rebuild what had been lost, without stopping or growing disheartened. To love a child meant to be there for him. To never give up. Robert smiled sweetly to himself.

The smile turned to a frown. Robert wasn't there for his own son. Instead, he was letting go of him as well as himself. Perhaps his son was waiting on the shoreline for him to come back, needing his support, expecting Robert to fill his bucket with joy. Robert surrendered to the massive wave that had destroyed his castle, letting it carry him far away.

***

"I hope I didn't keep you waiting too long," Jack said, approaching Robert from behind.

"It's okay," Robert replied, rising quickly and shaking the sand from his pants. "I was just enjoying this endless spectacle of nature. One thing I'm sure of is that I love the sea."

Jack stood beside him looking out at the view. "And I'm sure, in another life, I did, too," he replied wistfully. "You want to know something weird about this whole dimensional travel thing? This intertwining of lives and events? Well, I own an eighty-five-foot yacht. It's basically a mansion on the water. Something that the other Jack Redcliffe, the one I can't remember, apparently bought and used quite often. I assume that the other me, the one before the jump, loved the sea, too. From the photos I've seen, I even reached the Hawaiian Islands by boat several times. The ocean attracts me but scares me. When I'm close to the shoreline, my heart races and my temples pound. Each time, I back down and turn away."

"It's like living in the limbo of Dante's inferno," Robert said softly. "Ending up there without a verdict. Living in expectation, with the impossible hope to see God and finally get to know the truth."

Jack stared at him and tried to memorize those words. He felt his friend's pain alongside his own. Robert was right. He, too, had been living in a limbo, in that circle of hell that had given him no escape, no conclusion, nothing but a constant and eternal agony.

He looked away from Robert, trying to erase his sad and dramatic thought. "So, what did you want to talk to me about so urgently?" he said, changing the subject.

Robert was silent for a moment, gazing at his shadow stretched across the sand with his hands in his pockets. "I've decided."

"Decided what?" asked Jack with surprise.

Robert looked up and gave Jack a tender smile. "I decided to take the leap and go back. I want to try to take my life back into my own hands. Whatever it might be. Whatever the reason for my unhappiness there, I must try to put my life back together and give it meaning. And if Justin York's theory turns out to be right, then I—er, the other version of me that belongs here—will be able to make it work over here, too."

Jack heaved a sigh of relief. "How do you plan to do that? And, most importantly, when?"

The muscles in Robert's face tensed. "That's where you come into the picture."

***

That day, Susan left the hospital earlier than usual and rushed to the therapist's office. She had been meeting Dr. Freeman at 40 Central Park South for years. This time, she entered the doctor's office a different woman.

With Dr. Freeman, she had always discussed her daily problems, such as her difficulties with work, her family, and her husband. She had opened up about her mistakes and her regrets. She had asked for help in overcoming the pangs of guilt, the fears, and the weaknesses she was aware of. Today, she needed help to manage the overwhelming pain of Robert's impending death.

She knew she had made several mistakes in her marriage. She could have given more to him—he had always taken care of both her needs and Brian's. Several times, she had had difficulty being understanding and patient when facing family and relationship difficulties.

Robert had always been a sweet companion. She considered herself lucky to have had him as a husband all those years. But, at the same time, she felt guilty for how Robert's final hours were unfolding. The burden he had to bear.

She thought about the letter Robert had written a few hours before he ended up broken on the asphalt. In the days since the accident, she had wondered more than once if it had occurred because he was upset—whether he had wanted to end it all or if it was a simple moment of distraction caused by inner turmoil. Either way, she felt responsible. She would never have a chance to ask Robert what happened, nor would she be able to ask him for forgiveness.

By this point in her life, she had learned that what's done is done. What one does always remain part of their personal history. Time would not erase the memory, so trying to forget was of no use. The truth would always be there, waiting to reveal itself. On the contrary, trying to fix what went wrong was an act of honesty, a moment of courage and loyalty toward life.

Susan also thought of Brian's pain, the pain of a son who was unaware of what had happened between his parents. She thought about Robert's last emotions. About his sorrow. He was going to die, and his last memories would be of the worst moments in their relationship. The ugliness of those last years spent together. Her weakness.

She knew she could never reveal to Brian what had happened or she would lose him, too. Once again, she had no option but to ignore the facts. Hide the truth. Bury it somewhere deep with the hope that it would never be found again. She stepped into the elevator, looked at herself in the mirrored wall, and sobbed.

***

Jack held his tongue until Robert had fully explained his idea down to every detail. He knew his friend was hoping he would not refuse, but Jack's mind was flooded with a mixture of amazement and terror.

"No way!" he shouted, turning his back on him. "I can't do a thing like that. I couldn't even if I wanted to."

Robert had to have expected such a reaction. But Jack knew he was Robert's only chance, the only person who could save him, so guilt prickled him regardless.

"Jack, you're the only one who can do this," Robert urged. "You're the only one I trust and, more importantly, who trusts me."

"There must be another way," Jack replied, anguished. "I'm sorry."

Robert's expression turned pleading. "No, there is not. I couldn't think of anything else. And you know it, too. If you have a different idea, let me know. This is the only way to go if I want this to happen, and I can't do it all by myself. You must help me, please! You must be brave!"

The two were silent for a few moments.

Jack turned his gaze to the ocean, hypnotized by the continuous ebb and flow of the waves. Always the same, always changing. Always beautiful yet terrifying. "What if I were to fail?" he whispered at last. "What if I panic at the last minute? How can you trust me so much?"

Robert stared straight into his eyes. "The reason I decided to take the leap is because I want to take responsibility for my life. Dreams can't magically come true, as York says. You told me so, too, a few days ago. It's thanks to you, Jack, that I've been inspired not to run away from situations. As scary as it may be, I feel I have to do it. Of course, if it's not too late. Time was not kind to you, but you can still give meaning to your life. You'll be able to face your greatest fear and finally overcome it. I think this risk will do some good for you, too. It will be your chance." As he spoke, Robert's expression filled with mingled despair and hope.

Jack knew how true that torment was. No matter how excruciating, the time had finally come to make sense of it all—both for Robert's sake and his own. Meeting Robert was nothing short of destiny—a test. Perhaps it hadn't been accidental at all. In the end, a mysterious game of the universe had brought them together. In all of infinite time and space, Robert had wound up at Jack's restaurant. It was Robert who had come to him.

"You want me to help you die," Jack said slowly, "and then save you. By jumping back, you want to make things right here at the same time. But how will I know when it's time to bring you, the other Robert, back? What you're asking me is on the verge of murder."

"That's why we'll have to do it at sea. I can't count on a doctor to bring me to the edge of life or even ask one without risking being committed to an asylum. So the only *safe* way is for me to drown. Like I said, you'll take me out from the water the moment you notice I've lost consciousness. You'll revive me, the other Robert, with a cardiac massage. I know that, deep down, you are a man of the sea—both in this reality and likely in the other one. You'll know how to do it. And if you can't revive me, it means that at least I will have managed to jump back to my own reality, I hope . . ."

Jack tried to visualize the scene in his mind. He tried to convince himself that Robert was right, that it was possible. It had already happened for Justin York in a similar manner. "Okay, when do you think we should do this?" he asked with resignation.

"Tomorrow at dawn," Robert replied quickly, then added, "But only if I have the dreams tonight."

## XVII

That night, Robert and Patty ate a late dinner across from each other on the terrace.

"How are you today?" she asked tentatively.

"Good," he replied with some cheer. "Still waiting for my memory to return, but I'm feeling more positive about it."

Since the night before, the couple had not spoken much, wrapped in the embarrassment, guilt, and discomfort at the lack of trust they had learned they both had for each other.

In fewer than ten hours, Robert would attempt the jump. He wanted to confess many things to her, to say goodbye in case the other Robert couldn't be revived, in case that Robert would have no memories of these past several days. He wanted to tell her how much he loved her, though he was sure she knew it—even if she thought he was crazy. She knew how much he had loved her in those years in this reality. But she didn't know how much he had wanted her in the other one, too.

"Mosquito, there's something I want you to know," he said after a few moments.

Her grip tightened on her cutlery. "Tell me."

Robert gave her a reassuring smile and said, "Recent events have made me realize just how important you are to me. Even though I've had amnesia for these past six days, our love managed to remain my *only* memory. If anything should ever happen to me, know that my heart belongs to you. Even though you didn't believe that theory the other night, you have been and always will be my everything. No amount of time or space could ever stop me from loving you. I'm sorry for the suffering I've caused you and, if I ever inadvertently cause more pain in the future, I apologize for that too. The important thing is that you never forget that you are, and always will be, my mosquito."

Motionless, with the cutlery still clutched in her hands and her eyes swollen with tears, Patty listened to his words of love. Robert was sure she'd heard those words before over the years, that the Robert of this reality had never stopped telling her. But this night, it was different. He was a new and changed man—someone wounded to the depths of his soul, but one who could finally face her and say that his immense love for her had remained unchanged over time, despite the scratches of time itself and the pain.

"I love you too, Robert Lewis. I will always love you, no matter what. With or without memory. In sickness and in health, as I told you that day at that altar by the ocean. You are all I want, the only thing I need. You know that . . . or at least you did. Ever since those early days in in college, you have been the only man I've ever desired. What we're going through is just a test. We'll overcome it together."

Later, after dinner, they watched an hour of television before getting ready for bed. According to Patty, that was what they had always done all those years. He knew she saw this as getting back to normal, but Robert's mind was elsewhere. His plan began the moment he and Patty stepped into the bedroom. He had engineered everything down to the smallest detail. As he brushed his teeth at the bathroom mirror, he saw his hands shaking. He was scared — terrified that he would go to the edge of life to try to get back to living in both of these overlapping dimensions — and fail.

*What if it was like Patty had suggested?* he thought. What if he had become a crazy visionary who, after losing his memory for some unknown reason, needed to cling to nonsense theories? What if Jack, Justin York, and those nightmares were just a figment of his imagination — of his distorted and disturbed state of mind?

Robert shook those thoughts from his mind. He knew he was an intelligent man and that those doubts were caused by fear of the deed he would soon have to do.

He left the bathroom to find Patty already in bed with a book in her hand. She closed it, careful to bookmark the page, and placed it on her nightstand. He turned off the light. He shed his clothes and got under the sheets next to his wife. As he touched her body, Patty sighed and let him slowly take off her nightgown. They lay in the dark, listening to the ocean. Robert felt her skin on his own, and it felt familiar, like the sensation belonged to him. He felt her breath on his neck as he gave her pleasure. Her hands on his back. The scent of her hair. Everything was smooth and natural.

Robert willed Patty to feel all his passion in that moment, his love for her. Their bodies firmly joined together, and for a few moments, they lived for each other, as they always had in this reality.

Patty fell asleep naked in Robert's arms, but he couldn't get to sleep. He knew he had to fall asleep and wait for the dreams to come. That was the only way he could be certain that the Robert he had been was still alive. Otherwise, it would be foolhardy to carry out his plan. The more he tried to sleep, the more nervous he got. He tossed and turned, trying to find a comfortable position. He tried not to think. He let the sound of the waves envelope him. He absolutely had to fall asleep.

A nervous sweat still clung to his skin when sleep swept him away, and he found himself on that street corner again. The sunlight surprised him, while all around was chaos. The traffic light was still red. The scene was the same. He saw and heard the same people, the same voices. He even detected the same smells.

He stepped one foot down off the sidewalk and heard the car horns, followed by the screeching of tires on the asphalt. He saw the cab. He felt pain shoot through his body and closed his eyes.

When he opened them again, he was back in that dark room. From the window, a beam of light illuminated the silhouette of the young man sitting on a chair in front of him. He was no longer crying. He was just sad. His gaze was empty, as if he had just given up.

Robert tried to talk to him again. He shouted to make himself heard, but the young man didn't seem to notice.

Then Robert saw that there was another person sitting next to him. The homeless man in his other dreams. He was no longer standing on the street corner and didn't have a foul smell anymore. Robert wondered why the man was there and what the connection was between him and the younger man, his son. He wondered then where the woman was.

He winced in his sleep. Once, twice, three times. Until he opened his eyes again. He looked at his watch. It was half past three. He didn't have much time left. He tried to pull himself together and get up. He turned to Patty and saw that his nightmare had not woken her up. She was sleeping peacefully on her back, with one arm under his pillow and her curly black hair spread across her face.

Robert got up quietly and went into his study. He realized that he had only entered that room once since that first morning. On the wall to the right hung photos of him with various celebrities or holding trophies and awards. On the desk, next to the Mac, was an old typewriter. Patty had told him it had belonged to his grandfather. He recognized it. He remembered that as a child, he loved to sneak into the old man's office, where he pretended to write. He loved listening to the clanking sound as he tapped on the keys.

He turned on the lamp and sat down. Under the light of the desk lamp sat a small, framed picture of Patty and him. It was from their college days, she with the sunny smile that had never changed over the years, he with the long, messy hair.

He turned on his computer, opened a blank Word document, and began tapping on the keyboard, his mind set on everything he had thought about writing.

***

After receiving the long-dreaded phone call from Dr. Crown that morning, Susan and Brian made their way to the hospital.

It was raining. The cab carrying them had stopped right in front of a puddle, which Susan couldn't avoid as she got out, and she found her foot submerged in the muddy water.

"Dammit! Did you have to stop right here, asshole?" she yelled at the taxi driver.

Brian grabbed her hand to calm her down. "It's okay, Mom. It's nothing," he told her, reassuring her with a hint of a smile.

Once inside the hospital, they rode the elevator to the ICU floor. There, they were asked to sit in the room where Robert lay. They waited for Dr. Crown and his medical staff to join them so that they could start the process of shutting down the life-sustaining machine.

Brian and Susan sat in the two chairs from which they had been watching Robert for days. Brian saw Susan looked cast an irritated look at her muddy shoe and stiffen even more.

Robert's body lay on the bed in front of them. These would be the last moments Brian would have with his father, who was neither alive nor dead. He had always known that he would have to leave him one day. He just hadn't imagined that it would happen so soon and so tragically.

His dad wouldn't be there on his graduation day. He wouldn't attend his wedding. He would not know his grandchildren, if any. He would no longer comfort him in times of discouragement or help him in making important decisions. He wouldn't help him through the unbearable days to come.

His father would soon leave him for good. There would be no more hope. There would be no return. There would no longer be a miracle to pray for. For the past few, difficult days, Brian had kept the faith and thought the impossible could actually be possible. He had nearly convinced himself that his father would recover. It had never occurred to him that his father might leave him like this, without a final exchange of words.

After a few minutes, Dr. Crown entered the room, followed by two other physicians and a medical student. "Good morning," he said, his awkwardness palpable in that delicate moment.

"Good morning, Doctor," replied Brian and Susan.

The doctors consulted each other, whispering among themselves. They passed Robert's medical records from hand to hand. One of them stopped to explain to the young student what would happen soon.

Brian followed the scene with no emotion, his mind far away. Susan, on the other hand, kept her head down, her eyes fixed on her own clasped hands.

"So," Dr. Crown began, addressing Susan and Brian, "in a few moments we will disconnect the respirator and turn off the machines that have been keeping Robert's vital functions going. It will take a few minutes or a few seconds, then his heart will stop. Once we confirm his death, we will release Robert from the respirator, the electrodes, and the central venous catheter."

Brian nodded, listening to the doctor's voice as if it came from somewhere else, an echo coming from far outside of their living field.

"But first, we will leave you alone with Robert, so that you can say goodbye to him. We will then come back and start the procedure. Take all the time you need."

Dr. Crown gave Brian's shoulder a pat as he and his staff left the room.

***

At five o'clock in the morning, Robert sealed the two envelopes. One contained a letter was addressed to Patty, in which he reminded her how much he loved her in case "he" didn't make it back. The other one was addressed to Jack's attention. It contained a declaration of responsibility for the act he was about to perform — in essence, it was a suicide letter that Jack could use to exonerate himself if it came down to that.

He left Patty's envelope on the kitchen table and went to the walk-in closet, where he donned a bathing suit underneath a track suit and tennis shoes. He tucked Jack's letter in his pocket. He stole one last gaze at Patty, who was gratefully still sound asleep. He wanted to kiss her on the forehead one last time but didn't dare stirring her from sleep, and then he left the house.

He took a cab to the Balboa Yacht Basin in Newport, where Jack's boat had been docked for years. During the ride, he contemplated the choice he had made, what he was about to do, wondering if it was a senseless experiment. His desire to see the young man who had been crying for him for days was overwhelming. Leaving Patty was enormously difficult, and he pushed thoughts of her away. Instead, he reviewed the details of his plan.

The car proceeded slowly along the coast. While much of the world was still sleeping, the waves lapped on the shore as if locked in an endless struggle against the land, a struggle that was thousands of years old. As the cab reached the port, Robert saw Jack standing in the distance on the dock near his yacht. If things were different, he'd admire the yacht. For now, it represented an uncertain fate.

Robert hurried up and patted him on the back. "Ready, old man?" he asked, trying to appear calm.

Jack turned and gave him a hard stare. "Are you asking me if I'm ready to kill you? No."

Smiling despite the gravity of the situation, Robert noticed two young Hispanic men busy preparing the yacht for departure. "Who's that, Jack?"

"They work for me. They're coming with us."

"Are you crazy?" he demanded in a whisper.

"Look," Jack replied firmly. "You didn't think I could do this all by myself, did you? Plus, I trust these two guys. They are illegal immigrants who only speak Spanish. I've been supporting them financially for years along with their families. One of them claims he used to be a doctor in Mexico."

"Do you believe him?" asked Robert doubtfully.

"He's certainly not a chef. His cooking sucks!" said Jack, barking a laugh before his expression grew serious again. He looked at Robert. "Listen. We can't know if this leap into the void can really work. The fact it did with York doesn't guarantee that it will with you. From what we know, the transition happens at the precise moment one strongly desires to be elsewhere. That instant gets to be so close to death that it makes it almost impossible to bring back a person. I'm shitting in my pants. And not just because of that, but because I need to get on this damn boat. I've got a respirator and a defibrillator on board, but I need their help to pull you back up and try to revive you. I'm sure we'll need them."

Robert sighed.

"I assume you dreamed last night?" asked Jack.

"Yes. It was strange. I got the impression that I am very close to death on the other side."

"What made you think so?"

"I saw even more pain as well as a great resignation in the young man's eyes," Robert replied, staring at the wood grain of the floor, trying to divert his thoughts from the fear of no longer existing. "The dream has changed. I guess we don't have much time."

"It means we'd better get moving. But I have one more question to ask you before we head out to sea."

"Tell me," Robert said.

"How strong is your desire to go back right now?"

"It's more than a desire, it's a need. I need to get back to my son. I'm sure that's who he is. I intend to give him back what my dream took away from him. I want to bring order to the chaos I left in the past. I don't know what that other life is like, but I'm sure there would be no point in living here without having accomplished what I chose in that dimension. I'm ready to face the problem, whatever it is."

"What about Patty?"

Robert hesitated, then gathered his strength and answered. "I left her a letter. A letter I hope she doesn't need, if all goes according to plan. And if so, I will look for her in my other reality. If she's the one I wished for in death, then that means that's where I need to go to find her. Not here."

## XVIII

As the boat sailed, Jack clutched tightly to the taffrail. He couldn't remember the last time he had boarded that yacht, yet he could discern the emotions that were gripping his stomach. Once tried, no man could entirely forget the salty taste of the sea, the spray, and the changing colors that form as the bow carves its way through the waves.

They had agreed that they would move within a mile of the shoreline to enact the suicide dive. Robert had stripped down to his bathing suit.

Jack stood watching the sea for a long time. He followed its movements, the swells, the grooves and trails, in constant motion, like the thoughts of a man.

If Robert didn't come back or if the man he revived didn't remember the events of the past few days, he would miss him. Robert's recent presence had shed new light on his aimless and unvarying days. Though he had encountered many like him during his research, something about Robert felt special. In some way, helping him had given meaning to Jack's life in this dimension. Without Robert, he would be alone again. He watched Robert look around and gave one of the young crewmen the sign to turn off the engines.

From that point he could still see the shoreline in the distance. He could easily recognize The Cliff's sea-blue umbrellas and the area where Robert—the Robert of *this* dimension—and Patty had been living in the last few years.

"Okay!" Robert yelled. "This is where we're going to do it."

Jack and the two young men approached him.

***

Robert's plan was clear.

He would handcuff himself to the anchor with assistance. They would lower him into the water at an appropriate depth. In that way, he would not be able to climb back up when driven by the urge to survive. At the same time, he had to remain visible so he could be pulled out of the water in time.

They would wait for him to pass out. It would be a terrible moment for him; just imagining it, Robert felt his heart explode in his chest. The instant he became unconscious, he would be hauled back on board by Jack and his two companions, laid out on the deck of the boat, and resuscitated with CPR.

It was a very dangerous thing to do. Robert would gasp desperately for air, instinct taking over and forcing him to try and save himself. Once water entered his lungs and he ceased breathing, in the best-case scenario, he would lose consciousness without falling into a deep coma. Worst-case scenario, he'd die.

This second phase would last about a minute, and in that time, Jack would bring him back on board and revive him. The risk that Robert would reach the terminal stage and die from cardiac arrest was very high. In such case, he

187

would die, at least in this dimension. His life — both his lives — depended on a matter of seconds.

Robert would place his life in Jack's hands, and he knew Jack was terrified of what he had asked him to do. For the old millionaire, it was a crazy idea — a massive responsibility that Robert believed could be entrusted to no one else. Jack had even faced his terror of the sea, just to give his friend the chance he'd never had.

"Jack!" called Robert. "Here we go, my friend!"

"Here we go, yes . . ." replied Jack nervously.

"Before I dive in," Robert said, half-shouting to be heard over the wind, "I want to tell you something important. I want to thank you for what you have done — for what you are still doing now, for risking so much. You're a real friend, Jack — my Dante's Virgil in this dimension. If it weren't for you, I might never have known what happened to me. I would have gone crazy trying to figure it out. I would never have gotten any answers. You were not a random encounter in my life. Maybe all that's happened is fate. Maybe it's already been written. So if I don't make it, please don't feel guilty. It was all my work and my idea, no matter how reckless it is. But if I do survive, remind me that I owe you a martini at The Cliff."

Jack smiled. "Thanks to you, my friend! You've managed to make me feel alive again. And if I manage to keep myself from pulling you up too early, you'll owe me many martinis. Not just one."

At that point, Jack nodded to the two young men, who hurried to help Robert secure the handcuffs to the chain of a small anchor at the stern of the boat. After checking that everything was in order, they began to lower the end of the mooring into the water.

Robert stared at Jack for a few seconds, feeling as if time had stopped. He no longer felt the wind whirling around him nor the heave of the deck beneath his feet. His heart beat frantically, roaring in his ears. He tried to think again of the reason for this madness. The love for Patty, for his supposed son, and for life itself.

With trepidation, he looked down at the water below him. Then he smiled at Jack, who returned his smile with tenderness.

"Robert, if you make it to the other side, please do me a small favor."

"Anything!" Robert replied as he began to lean out of the boat.

"Go see Maria Sanuti. For sure she was the love of my life, probably my wife," Jack said, and for the first time in many years, a tear ran down his face, "and tell her I loved her so much, in every dimension of this crazy universe!"

Robert agreed by a slight tilt of his head. Jack nodded at the two men.

***

Susan and Brian stood at Robert's bedside, lost in thoughts of times long past and memories that would remain in their lives forever, when Dr. Crown and his staff entered the room again.

Crown offered a sympathetic smile as he waited for them to step aside so that he could start performing the delicate and agonizing operation. He began typing on the control panel of the machine. He inhaled deeply before pressing the "off" button. He turned toward Brian for only a moment, but to Brian, that paused seemed eternal.

A tear slid down Brian's face. Only one, single tear. The last tear of hope and the first one of pain. The beep of the machine and the fan pump were interrupted by a click that echoed through the room. In Brian's ears, that sound became a deafening noise. With a sigh, Susan brought her hands to her face to cover her weeping. Brian placed a hand on his mother's shoulder and hugged her, holding her close. His stoic expression transformed into a grimace of pain.

***

Once fully submerged in the chilly ocean waters, Robert tried to hold his breath. After almost a minute, he began to let go and swallowed salt water. He struggled, but his wrists were firmly attached to the chain. He imagined he could see Jack watching from above the water, trembling, waiting to give the men the signal to pull him up. Another thirty seconds passed — thirty interminable seconds before Robert's body stopped wriggling like a fish trying to free itself from the hook that had entangled it with deception.

At that moment, Robert's thoughts went to that young man in tears, to the desire to comfort him. He wished for his old life back with whatever problems he'd have to mend. He thought about Patty, the one he had left twenty years ago. He felt certain he would see her on the other side.

He would do everything possible to find her again and make up for his mistakes. He thought of how desperate he must have been to have wished with such determination to be somewhere else, about the regret he had felt that had in turn projected him into another dimension.

He found himself in absolute darkness. The water in which he was immersed suddenly felt like fire. It was as if thousands of needles were piercing into his flesh. At that point, Robert stopped struggling, his body jerked a few more times before he went still. Lifeless.

***

Jack signaled to pull him up. The most critical moment had arrived. They had to resuscitate him, make him breathe again. They had one chance to bring him back to life in this dimension, hoping that the same thing would happen in the other one.

The three men hauled up the anchor chain, bringing Robert's limp body back on board. They immediately laid him on the deck of the boat.

"Stay with me, my friend!" Jack yelled in desperation, as he grabbed the two electrodes of the defibrillator and placed them on his chest. "Don't even think about leaving me now!"

As soon as Dr. Crown turned off the machine and removed the breathing tube, silence filled the room, broken only by Susan's desperate and inconsolable crying. Brian continued to hold her, staring at his father's lifeless body when suddenly he noticed it shudder. His eyes widened in shock.

Robert's mouth opened wide and a gloomy, deafening scream tore out of him. His eyes flew open, and he began to cough convulsively, petrifying the onlookers. He lifted his head off the pillow for a moment and then let it fall back again, where he remained, staring at the ceiling and breathing heavily.

Gripped with terror, Susan had stopped sobbing. Brian rushed to his father's side. His eyes were wide open, his chest frantically expanding and relaxing.

Robert was alive. He had come back to life.

Dismayed, the medical staff did not know how to react to what was happening. Dr. Crown stood motionless, visibly confused.

"Dad!" shouted Brian finally.

***

Robert turned his tired gaze to his son. He recognized him immediately. He tried to smile but lacked the strength.

"Mr. Lewis, blink if you can hear me," stammered the doctor, staggering toward the bed.

Robert slowly closed and opened his eyes again.

"Mr. Lewis, you are in the hospital right now. You were involved in a bad accident and have been in a coma for six days."

Robert looked briefly at Brian again, and then went back to stare at the ceiling. He had been in a coma for six days. He had been on that bed for six days. He managed a trembling smile. All of what had happened came back to him.

## XIX

Days would pass before the doctors discharged Robert from the hospital. He would have to wear a brace on his right leg. The abrasions on his back from skidding across the pavement still caused him excruciating pain. Brian and Susan visited him every day. Bouquets of flowers poured in from his colleagues at the law firm, as well as from his many clients, his friends, and his family.

Six days earlier, he had been on the corner of Madison Avenue and 59th Street. Frustrated and distraught, he had attempted to cross against the traffic light. He was hit by a cab. In the accident, he was thrown to the sidewalk, where he landed on a homeless man sitting on the edge, begging for money. On impact, the homeless man had broken his neck, and he'd died after five days of agony in the same hospital, two rooms down from Robert's.

Robert could now piece together all the connections in his dreams. His tearful son, the woman with the smudged lipstick, who was the wife he had wanted to leave, the homeless man involved in the accident, and the busy intersection where everything had happened. It all added up.

He and Susan hadn't spoken much since his awakening. During visiting hours, they had often been silent, each engaged in reading. Sometimes they would talk about trivial things. For Susan, he knew not being able to discuss important topics with him made her feel uncomfortable.

Susan had masterfully avoided the subject of the letter. For his part, Robert had decided that he would talk to her about it once he was out of the hospital.

As soon as he was alone in his room, Robert enjoyed listening to the noises coming from the street. From there he could hear the cars honking, the sirens of police patrols or ambulances whizzing through the city, the voices of passers-by, or the screams of some lunatics. But his mind always went back to his few days with Patty by the ocean, a totally different dimension from the one he had returned to.

He could still hear the crashing of the waves and the cries of the seagulls. He remembered the sunlight spreading into their home, filling every corner. He thought of Jack and wondered if, in the end, he had been able to save him — if the Robert in the other reality had managed to get back into Patty's arms or if he had died by drowning. Maybe in that moment, in a place that was so far away in time and space, his woman, his wife in that parallel life, was crying for him, destroyed by the pain and the thought that everything had happened because of a quick-onset and irreversible mental problem.

In those days, he had also feared that he might have just dreamed everything — one of those dreams that happens to people in a coma. Some of them were of seeing the light. Others were of meeting people who had been deceased for years. Then there were those, like him, who were dreaming of waking up in a different dimension. But as Justin York had said, it all felt so vividly real.

Whatever it was, dream or no dream, what had happened had opened his eyes. It had made him realize the importance, the ultimate value, and the very meaning of life itself. His own life. It had made him review and reevaluate the choices, right and wrong, that he had made. It had made him rediscover the importance of being a father. The importance of love. How indispensable Patty had been for him.

The day before, he had asked Brian to bring him his iPad. He decided to find Patty. He needed to know where she was, what she was doing, and most importantly, if she was alive. He was determined to find her and reunite with her. He typed her full name into Google. Patricia Down. The results of his online search yielded little information. They were about her college years, the seminars she had attended, and a few pictures from her graduation day. Nothing more.

He didn't give up, searching for information by scanning social media profiles. He looked for the name of people he remembered being Patty's friends from college. At one point, he found a photo of her on the Facebook page of a mutual friend, Francesca. All the people in the picture had been tagged. Among them was Patty. She was no longer called Patricia Down, but Patricia Carlton. She had married.

Robert sighed in distress. He suddenly felt stupid for not having considered that option. Like him, after their relationship ended, she had rebuilt her life. She had fallen in love and married.

From further information, he learned that Patricia Carlton had become a well-known painter. Robert suddenly remembered that, indeed, painting had been one of Patty's passions when she was young. Evidently, she must have pursued her dream. She held exhibitions all over the world and was living in Los Angeles with her husband, Paul Carlton, a wealthy plastic surgeon.

From those pictures, Robert inferred that his Patty was a happy woman who was satisfied with her life. She still had she same smile and looked like the Patty he had met in those days in Laguna Beach. In this life, her hair was straight, but her smile and the little wrinkles on her skin made her look just the same.

Robert decided that the fact that she was married wouldn't stop him from trying to get together with her. He hadn't stopped when he had to face the entire universe. He would not stop now, just because she was married.

He needed to see her and to apologize to her. He was the one who had decided to leave her and go to New York. It was he who had taken that flight and, by doing so, had changed both their destinies. But there was a place where they were still together. In another dimension, they were together, and they were happy. He hoped.

From her official website, he read that she would exhibit her work at the Exposition Park in Los Angeles a month from that day. He decided that would be the place he would meet her again.

***

Robert was discharged from the hospital on a sunny morning. New York in the spring was a starburst of color, the air was crisp, the temperature mild, and new life sprouted up everywhere. *The only season with truly likable weather*, he thought as he looked from the window at the many cars and cabs jostling down Park Avenue.

The night before, he had hardly been able to sleep, grappling with what was real and what wasn't. The logical side of his brain debated with the more open-minded part of him that the alternate dimension had just been an elaborate coma-induced dream. Logic had the stronger argument.

As Robert stood with his gaze lost beyond the window, Dr. Crown entered the room. "Good morning, Mr. Lewis."

Robert turned and answered with a nod.

"I really must say, this was definitely what many consider a miracle," the doctor said as he consulted the medical records.

Robert sat on the bed and let Dr. Crown examine him for the last time. "I'd like to ask you something, Doctor," said Robert, trying to stay as still as possible.

"Of course, Mr. Lewis. Go ahead."

"I would like to pay for the funeral for the homeless man who lost his life because of me in that terrible accident. Could you help me with that?"

"Sure," replied the doctor, shining a small flashlight into Robert's eyes. "Interestingly, that man was a disgraced millionaire. While trying to determine if he had any family, we found out that his name was Justin York, a lottery winner. There was an accident at sea, which he survived, but he had serious mental problems. He lost everything."

Robert felt his heart skip a beat. "Did you say Justin York?" he asked with astonishment.

"That was his name, correct. His body is still lying in the morgue. It has been waiting for someone as generous as you to decide to give him a proper burial."

Robert's mind filled with a thousand, crazy thoughts. The same thing might happen to the other Robert. Even though he had been rescued by Jack, in his other dimension, he might have lost all control and awareness of reality. The thought terrified him. But, as he had thought the night before, the Robert who had risked drowning would never know. Nor would the Justin York he'd met in Phoenix. Robert's logical mind shouted at him, *Get a grip!*

As Dr. Crown finalized the last report for his discharge form, Robert walked over to the chair next to the bed and let himself fall into it. He took his iPad. He typed the name Jack Redcliffe into Google and waited to see what came up. He found him among all those with the same name.

Jack had been a professional diver involved in many operations to recover historical underwater artifacts. He had explored the seabed of many seas. And had ended up in a coma due to an embolism some twenty years earlier, during a dive in Portugal in search of an old Spanish vessel that had sunk in the sixteenth century, carrying a cargo of gold from the New World.

He had been in a vegetative state for about a year before his wife, Maria Redcliffe, had disconnected him from life support. Robert even found a eulogy she had written in memory of her husband. It mentioned the enchantment and pain of a woman in love. Theirs had been an everlasting love that had begun in their high school days and ended tragically.

Robert read the article carefully, until he was struck by another strange coincidence that sent a chill down his spine. Jack's wife had donated to Lenox Hill Hospital, the same one where Robert was. In turn, the hospital had dedicated one of its operating rooms to Jack.

Robert dropped the iPad on his lap and looked up at the ceiling. He couldn't explain all those coincidences. Robert seriously considered the possibility that during his coma, someone had mentioned the name of the homeless man who had died in the accident. His mind had associated these names with his jumbled memories, such as his marital problems, Patty, his passion for writing, and his love for the ocean. Everything had blended into one incredible dream.

Suddenly he felt stupid. Had he really believed that there could be alternate dimensions? That somewhere in the universe, there was another Robert Lewis, who was simultaneously living another life? Yes. The truth was that part of him truly believed he had made a space-time leap and had awakened next to the woman he had loved twenty years before. Robert smiled sadly into the void. As absurd as it was, he liked to believe he had taken the leap. But whether he had imagined it or had really lived it, the experience, the dream, had changed him. He had found the determination to change his life. Take it into his own hands and make it real. Give it more value.

Robert had become different. He could feel it. He understood that life—this one life he had—was not a dream.

## XX

The black car carrying Susan, Robert, and Brian stopped in front of their building on the corner of Park Avenue and 60th Street, about fifteen blocks from the hospital where Robert had been hospitalized for several weeks.

Just as they arrived on the twenty-fourth floor and the elevator door slid open, they found their neighbor Carla standing in front of them.

As the woman gave Robert a sweet hello and expressed her happiness at seeing him safely home after that tragic accident, Susan rushed to open the door. Her hand was shaking so much that it seemed like she had taken the wrong key. She managed to open the door, and she watched Robert smile at his neighbor before he followed her and Brian into the house.

Brian helped his father unpack his few belongings while Susan hurried to prepare a pasta salad for lunch. Once seated at the table, just before picking up the cutlery, Robert said he needed to make an announcement.

Brian and Susan stopped and listened.

"I decided to take a step back from work," he declared. "I'd rather devote myself to what I have always wanted to do, which is to write a novel."

There were a few moments of silence.

"I think that's a wonderful idea, Dad!" Brian exclaimed with excitement.

Susan remained silent. Her legs trembled under the table. She knew there was still something they should talk about. That moment was coming up. Robert's detachment was a sign. He was hurt, and she was terrified of losing him. The problem was that letter—that one flaw in their life together, which she believed had been forgotten. Almost forgotten. A rift in the framework of their splendid relationship. A small crack that had been threatening to bring everything down.

Susan watched as Brian animatedly chatted with his father about his plans. Her heart clenched over how much her son had suffered while Robert had been on the brink of death. She knew that if she and Robert failed to save their marriage, Brian would be heartbroken. It was the last thing she wanted.

During the rest of the lunch, father and son took the opportunity to talk about various possible ideas for a novel. Robert told Brian about his youth, when he loved to write short prose and poetry and how he had decided to leave San Diego after graduation to move to New York for law school. He told him about his passions, his friends, and his family.

Susan realized how much the accident had changed her husband. Robert usually didn't talk about his past. Now, he had decided to leave his job, ending the career he had built with such tenacity. From one day to the next, he was letting everything go in order to write, to follow the passion he had harbored since he was a teenager.

He was different a man. She wondered if that change was also because of the sad truth that had come into light the day of his accident.

That afternoon, Brian said goodbye to his parents and went back to campus to continue the studies that he had interrupted to be near his father, hugging them both on the way out.

Once alone, Robert and Susan sat on the sofa. Their gazes didn't meet as he stared into the void.

Susan took a deep breath and said, "I think we should talk, Robert. I know how you feel, and I'd like to explain myself to you. I'd like to tell you everything."

Finally, he turned to look at her. The grimace on his face laid bare all the disappointment and resentment he was feeling for her. "What would you like to explain to me? That you had an affair with our neighbor? That not only did you cheat on me for years with someone I met every day in the elevator, but also that you did it with a married man? Carla's husband? How do you manage to make eye contact with her every time you meet her on the landing? How could you do that to me?"

Susan's eyes filled with tears.

As he had explained briefly in his letter to her, weeks earlier, when the painters were working on the walls of the apartment, Robert had noticed the old security camera pointing at the front door. He had installed it when they bought the apartment years before, and since then, he had forgotten its existence. Out of sheer curiosity, he had viewed its contents by plugging it into the computer in his office.

That's how he'd learned about it. In those images, from three years earlier, Susan repeatedly greeted their neighbor at the door with passionate kisses that often smeared her lipstick. This was at a time when Robert had had to travel frequently for a rather demanding legal case, one that had forced him several times to spend entire weeks in Washington, D.C.

It was proof of Susan's betrayal. The reason for the end of their neighbors' marriage. Carla found out that her husband was cheating on her. She never knew with whom he had cheated. She had found a farewell letter addressed to her husband, an anonymous letter written by a woman. A woman whose identity had never emerged, not even after the divorce.

The man had hidden Susan's identity until the end. But Robert was meant to find out anyway.

"You've kept this secret all these years. You smiled at that woman every day. You kissed me and declared your love and loyalty to me every day, in all this time. How could you?"

Susan had been silent the entire time. Tears streaming down her face, she looked pleadingly at her husband. She didn't reply. There was nothing to say, nothing that could undo that mistake, nothing that could repair the damage that had been done. She had lied to, betrayed, and disrespected him.

The moment had come that she had to deal with her choices. The past would not forget, no matter how deeply the truth had been buried.

"I want a divorce," Robert concluded, as he stood up from the couch and disappeared behind the bedroom door.

Robert placed his laptop on the table facing a glass window overlooking the ocean. He had decided to stay in the Hamptons, leaving Susan alone in the city, in their apartment on Park Avenue. She hadn't objected to his decision. She had accepted the consequences of her actions without a fight.

He switched on his MacBook Air and stared at the Atlantic Ocean stretching in front of him. This view held a different allure from the one he had seen in his dreams. There, the light was brighter and warmer, with vibrant colors that created warmth and harmony. This panorama before him was a stormy and restless one, one that filled him with anxiety.

On the beach, he spied Brian running and playing with Jack, the German shepherd Robert had adopted to keep him company in his new life as a single man.

Brian had helped him move and was staying with him for a while. Robert and Susan decided it was better that he didn't know the real reasons behind their split. Brian hadn't taken it too hard, as having his father back from near death was relief enough for him.

After watching Brian and Jack playing on the beach for several minutes, he suddenly remembered the dream he had weeks before, when another father and his little boy were building sandcastles on a beach. Robert felt he owed his son all the love he had, his full support, and constant reassurance. This was a father's role.

Dream or no dream, Robert was back. He had woken up again for him — for Brian. At that moment, Brian turned to the window and waved to his smiling father.

That evening, after Brian had joined some friends at a nearby club, Robert sat down again in front of his computer and booked a flight to Los Angeles for the next day. Patty's exhibition would start in two days. He would show up on the opening day. He didn't have a plan. He just wanted to see Patty and talk to her. He *needed* to see her.

He also booked a room at the USC Hotel, a short walk from the exhibit.

The thought of his college sweetheart made his heart beat faster. Dream or no dream, what had happened to him had made him realize that there was something unfinished in his life. Something important had been left behind in the past, something unresolved.

They hadn't so much as spoken to one another in years, too hurt by the repercussions of his decision to leave to maintain even a friendship. Then he'd met Susan, and he'd fallen in love again. He had thought he was happy. He had thought *they* were happy. Instead, in all those years, he had simply been burying the regret of that difficult and obviously wrong choice.

***

The plane took off on time from JFK Airport.

Robert sat in his business-class window seat. As he looked out, he thought about the dream he'd had of that helicopter flight with Jack. His memory of it was still so

207

vivid in his mind. The desert below, the red sand of Phoenix, and the excitement of the flight—it had all seemed so real to him.

Robert had brought a book to read for the duration of the flight, *Love in the Time of Cholera* by Gabriel Garcia Marquez. Though it was technically a romance novel, he'd chosen it when he read the marketing copy. The similarity between the book's plot and his personal situation was striking. The only difference was that, unlike Fermina's husband, Patty's husband was still alive and that perhaps she was happy in the relationship with him.

There was also a chance she would barely remember him. Robert considered that in the end, the trip could turn into an awkward experience. But first and foremost, he felt that he owed it to himself. He needed to see her again, if only for a minute. He needed to understand how he still felt about her, whether that dream had been some sort of a premonition.

When the pilot announced the plane was beginning its descent, Robert put the seat back in the upright position and looked through the window again. As the plane descended over the illuminated streets, Robert thought once more of Justin York's words (or at least the ones he had fabricated), his clear vision of life and living—the difference between dreams that never came true and those in which one had truly believed.

He reminded himself that life should be lived fully, not allowed to go to waste.

***

The cab wended slowly through the city traffic. It was a hot and muggy day. The sun scorched the asphalt. On the side of the streets, bare-chested homeless men protected themselves from the blazing heat underneath cardboard boxes.

He thought with sadness of the poor homeless man—Justin York, he remembered with a shiver—who had died as a result of his accident.

Just before arriving at its destination, the cab slowly drove past Exposition Park. A colorful banner hung from a nearby building, advertising the upcoming exhibition. The name Patricia Carlton appeared in large letters above the background of a painting with a sun, whose colors faded away from the center, deep crimson blending gradually outward to pale yellow that all but faded into the white background. It was very similar to the painting Patty had given him in college. Patty had explained to him that he had been her inspiration, that he was like the sun to her. When they were apart, the sun faded and she felt chilled.

Patty had never stopped painting the sun. Maybe she hadn't forgotten about him, after all.

Anxiety twisted in his stomach. He tried not to think too much about it. Soon, he would know everything. The moment their eyes locked, everything would become clear. He would understand if that sun still burned for him. He would know if, in seeing him, she felt that heat again. Soon, he would know for certain.

The cab pulled up in front of the hotel. After checking in, Robert locked himself in his room. The opening would be the following day. He felt the need to rest. He walked into the bathroom and undressed. He was about to slip into the shower when he paused to observe himself in the mirror. It had been a long time since he had done so. He realized how much he had aged over the years.

In those college days, all he had thought about was Patty and him together. About their youth. Now, in front of that mirror, he realized how much time had passed since then. He studied his crow's feet and the lines in his forehead, the slightly sagging skin around his jawline. The shape of his eyes, which Patty had liked so much, was no longer the same; his eyelids had relaxed into a sort of sad and tired expression.

It took a lot more imagination than Gabriel Garcia Marquez's to hope that she could still see him as a handsome man, the way he used to be. With that daunting thought, he stepped into the shower, the roar of the water as it rushed over his ears reminding him of an ocean plunge.

## XXI

Robert took one last look at his reflection before leaving his room, adjusting the navy tie he had layered with a dark blue suit and white shirt.

A barber not far from the hotel had trimmed his hair that morning. He felt like a teenager getting ready for prom night. Only in this case, the girl he intended to see still didn't know who would be joining her. His leg still hurt, but he had decided not to use the brace. The bruises on his face and body had now healed. He took one long breath and left the hotel room.

He had decided to walk to the exhibition. As he arrived in front of the Exposition Park facility, he saw the red carpet leading from the sidewalk to the building, through the glass front door. A few photographers were taking turns capturing images of the guests as they arrived. On one side a few feet away stood a huddle of journalists and photographers, all following the press conference that preceded the ribbon cutting.

That's when he saw her. Patty. She was dressed in a white flowing dress that hugged her waistline and dipped into a vee at her neck. Her straightened hair fell softly over her shoulders. Her smile was unmistakable, as sunny as the heart of her paintings. Robert watched as she gestured and spoke to the reporters with amazing confidence. Every time she smiled, everything around her lit up.

He had just stepped onto the red carpet when he realized how visibly nervous he was. He looked at his trembling hands. "Cut it out, Robert," he whispered to himself. "You're just seeing your ex-girlfriend. Nothing bad can happen."

As he got closer, that nervousness grew.

The press conference ended when he was almost in front of the entrance, where Patty cut the ribbon to formally open the event and posed for the flashing cameras. All those present applauded and followed her inside the building.

Once inside the facility, Robert lost sight of her. A waiter holding a tray of champagne stopped in front of him. Robert took one of the crystal flutes and walked over to the nearest paintings.

The main subject of each canvas was the sun, Patty's distinct signature. Some paintings were brighter than others. Some gave a sense of warmth. Others exuded anguish and coldness, as if the sun's presence wasn't enough to enliven them, as if it were too distant to provide any warmth anymore.

Robert stopped in front of a painting resembling the one she had given to him, twenty years earlier. He studied at it in detail and thought back to the sweetness of that day. She had shown up at the door of his campus dormitory, holding that small painting swathed in wrapping paper. He recalled the kisses they'd exchanged right after, lying on the bed as they gazed at the painting hanging on the opposite wall, and the meaning she had given to it.

"This is definitely my favorite," said a female voice behind him.

He turned around and found himself face to face with Patty.

Seeing him, she almost dropped the glass she was holding. He smiled at her.

"Robert!" she exclaimed, her expression dumbfounded. "What are you doing here?"

"Hi, Patty. I was in town and happened to read about your exhibit. I thought, why not?"

"Oh, my goodness! It's so nice to see you again."

"It's nice to see you too, Patty. Or should I call you Mrs. Carlton?"

She smiled awkwardly. A young man, a member of the exhibition staff, approached, looking for her attention.

Patty laid a hand on Robert's arm. Her touch electrified him.

"Excuse me one second—please don't leave! As soon as I have some breathing room, I want to hear all about you, what you've been doing. Stay." Having said so, she followed the young man away.

***

A couple of hours passed before the exhibit guests began to leave.

Robert passed the time talking to an interesting cast of characters. Los Angeles was a very different city from New York. In Los Angeles, one could meet uber-successful people from the entertainment industry as well as those who were still chasing dreams of fame in the same place.

People flaunting wealth and extravagance and young, offbeat artists all gathered together.

As he downed the last sip of his second flute of champagne, Patty approached him.

This time, she was smiling happily. Her eyes shone with surprise and contentment. "Sorry to keep you waiting," she said. "I hope you don't have any other plans because I really would like to spend some time together and hear everything about you!"

Robert smiled at her. "To tell you the truth, I flew all the way to Los Angeles from New York just to be here," he confessed. "I read about your exhibit and jumped on the first flight."

Patty laughed. "Are you kidding me? Seriously, what are you doing in Los Angeles?"

"I am not kidding, and the reason I decided to do so could surprise you even more."

Patty stopped smiling and turned serious. "Robert . . ." she whispered.

"I know you're married," he assured her. "Maybe even happy. Don't worry, I'm not here for some crazy reason. I'm not here to convince you to run away with me or something — nothing like that. Truth is, I had an accident a few weeks ago and ended up in a coma for six days, during which I had one of those dreams that you hear about from people who have had the same experience. A dream that was so clear, it seemed almost real."

"Oh my God, Robert, I'm so sorry." She clutched his arm. "How do you feel now? What dream?"

"I dreamed I was in another life, in another dimension. There, I had not taken that flight to New York. My life was with you. We were together. We were happy. It made me realize how important you had been in my life. How important you still are. And I had to come and tell you. It was as if, since that departure, I had left something unfinished. Something unsaid. Thanks to that dream, I could see clearly how my life had been changed by that choice. I owed it to myself to come and see you. I owed it both to you and to myself."

Although Patty's expression was most composed, her lips trembled with emotion. "Robert, you were the most important man in my life. My first love. No one ever came close to you. Your decision to leave was an unbelievable pain that I carried with me for years. Obviously, I moved on. But I never forgot about you. I didn't try to make you stay. I didn't do it because I knew you. You needed to be free, to take off. You deserved it. You were very mature for you age, and you made a mature man's choice. I felt I was the obstacle that was holding you back. My love for you, in that moment, was greater than my love for the two of us together."

Robert stood riveted in place, dumbfounded. He remained there even as Patty stepped away to bid some of her guests goodbye. Everything she'd said, every pain she'd experienced and fear she'd felt—he'd felt the same things. His empty champagne flute trembled in his hands.

***

As soon as Patty said goodbye to the last guest, and the facility was nearly empty, she and Robert left together. She explained that her husband was on business elsewhere.

They walked down the street in search of a bar to sit and talk. They finally settled on Rock & Reilly's, an Irish pub that looked decent enough. They chose a table near the window that looked out onto the adjacent street. They gazed at each other in silence for a while before the waiter arrived to take their order. They both decided on a pint of beer.

They spent hours happily reminiscing about the past they had shared, such as when Robert slipped off a cliff one afternoon when they had taken a hiking trip in the mountains, or when Patty's overly curly hair got caught in the watch on his wrist, forcing them to cut off a strand to free her. Both sighed at every memory. It had been a good time in their lives.

After finishing her studies, Patty had devoted herself to what she most loved, which was painting. Over the years, when she had become a highly celebrated painter, she had moved to Los Angeles, where she'd met her current husband.

"Are you happy?" Robert asked her, point blank.

Patty felt the full weight of that unexpected question. She inhaled and held back the words, as if she wanted to select them properly first. "I've come to a point where I believe that the kind of happiness we see in movies or read about in books, in reality, doesn't exist. Compromises, yes, those do exist. I don't mean that we have to accept something that we don't like. If anything, we should settle for something that is a few steps below happiness. I don't know anyone in Los Angeles who is truly happy in their private relationship. When I look at them, I consider myself lucky."

"I see," Robert replied, fiddling with the coaster in front of him.

"My marriage is pretty much at the end of the road," Patty went on. "It's been a difficult few years. My husband and I slowly drifted apart, and now I no longer see the reasons why and how we ended up getting married. We are talking about divorce, but I don't want to give you any false illusions. It was very nice between us, but I am no longer the woman I used to be back then. That naive and generous girl you knew — It's better to leave the good memories where they belong, in the past."

Robert nodded. Patty's words made sense. Each of them had inevitably changed during all those years.

"Robert . . . remember the nickname you called me back then?"

"Mosquito."

"And do you remember why?"

He smiled. "You reminded me of it in my dream."

She gave him a quizzical look, and then she laughed, darting a glance at her Cartier watch. Her eyes widened.

It was almost midnight.

"Gosh, it's so late!" she exclaimed. "I can't remember the last time I was out this late!"

Robert smiled. "You didn't notice because you had a nice time."

She took his hand, which had been resting on the small table. "It was very nice, indeed. I'm glad we got together again. And I think you were right to look for me. It was good for both of us. Knowing how stubborn you are, I guess it took a coma to make you decide to do it."

He laughed heartily. "Yes, Patty. It was good I did it. Seeing you again was important. You were the greatest love for me, too. And when I found myself at the crossroads of life and death, you were the one who came to my mind. That must mean something."

She gave him a small nod and squeezed his hand.

Once outside the club, Patty raised her arm, and seconds later a blue car with a yellow roof pulled up in front of them. "Do we get in together or would you rather wait for another one?"

"I'm staying at the USC Hotel, a few blocks from here. I can walk from here."

She peered at him and gave him a smile. He smiled back.

They spent a few seconds staring at each other until Patty moved closer and hugged him tightly before kissing him on the lips. "Maybe we'll meet again in another life, and everything will be different."

Robert smiled again. "Yes, maybe in another dimension."

"Who knows!" she replied amusedly, ducking inside the cab.

Robert watched from the sidewalk as the cab drove away down West Jefferson Boulevard. He smiled again to himself. He was suddenly alone, in the dark of the night. "Now I'm ready to write my first novel," he mumbled.

***

Once in his hotel room, Robert slowly undressed, turning over in his mind the beautiful evening he had spent with Patty. She was at the end of an unhappy marriage, while he had crossed that line a few weeks earlier.

She had also told him that now she was a different woman. But when he looked into her eyes, he found the same kind soul. She was the same sweet Patty, sensitive but strong—the same woman he had seen in his dream, who tried in every way to help him regain his memory. The same woman who, in that other "life," had wanted to save their marriage.

Shirtless, he pressed a hand to his wounded leg and grimaced. He was about to undo his pants when he heard a knock at his door.

Confused, he instinctively looked at his watch. It was 12:45 a.m. He went to the door and opened it.

Patty stood before him, holding a bottle of champagne and two glasses. Her face lit with a smile. "I thought that since you're only here until tomorrow, why not enjoy your visit to the West Coast until the end?"

Caught by surprise, Robert stared at her without saying a word.

"Well? Are you going to invite me in, or are you just going to stand there showing off your aging abs all night?"

# XXII

Patty sat at the kitchen table, facing the window overlooking the ocean.

In one hand, she clutched in quiet desperation the letter Robert had left on the kitchen table for her, earlier that morning.

*I have loved you from the day I laid eyes on you, and I will love you for all eternity. You are my everything, mosquito. I know how difficult these past few days have been for you. I desperately want to be here for you with all my memories intact, but if for some reason, I cannot be there for you, if I cannot be by your side moving forward, please forgive me. Do not waste your days in sadness or regret. Live your life to the fullest for both of us. I have and will always treasure your love and devotion.*

Patty brought first a hand to her lips, then to the tears streaming inconsolably from her eyes. She stared at the boundary between sea and sky, which had suddenly emptied itself of the meaning she had always given it.

It wasn't easy for her to figure out what Robert had decided to do. She didn't know where he was at that moment. She was exhausted by what had happened in those few fraught days. Everything had fallen apart, like a house of cards collapsing in front of her.

"No!" she shouted at last. "No, no, no!"

She got up and raced to the window, striving in vain to see Robert down there, among the people on the endless beach. Then, clutching the letter tightly in her hands, she fled the house, hurried down the steps that led to the beach, and started running blindly, tears blurring her vision.

She staggered to the shoreline. Holding the letter tightly to her chest, she screamed at the sky. It was as if a part of her being had been torn away. Her heart was leaving her. Her great love. Falling to her knees, she stared desperately out to sea as her tears spattered the sand beneath her.

***

Jack placed the electrode pads on Robert's bare chest, causing him to jolt. He hit them a second time, then a third one.

"Come on, man. Don't do this to me!" he said frantically, darting a glance at the man giving Robert's mouth to mouth. "Come on, Robert! Come back to life!"

He dialed up the voltage slightly on the defibrillator and tried again.

On the fourth blast, a stream of water came out of Robert's mouth. Then another.

Jack held still, waiting for further small signs of life.

Robert vomited more water and began to cough. The three men turned him on his side to prevent the water and vomit from blocking his airways.

"Come on, dude!" Jack exclaimed. "You've made it! Good boy! Good boy!"

Jack and his two helpers tried to sit Robert up. One man grabbed him from under his arms and the other put the oxygen mask over his mouth.

"Holy crap, Robert, I can't believe it!" said Jack excitedly, sitting down on the deck in front of him. "You're alive, man! You gave me such a scare! I swear, if you ask me to do anything like that again, I'll leave you down there next time!"

At first Robert looked confused, and then he smiled from behind the oxygen mask. The smile slowly turned to laughter and coughing.

"What are you laughing at, you fool!?"

Robert was now laughing convulsively, clapping his hands and looking up at the clear sky above them. He just couldn't seem to stop laughing.

"What's going on, man?" Jack demanded, puzzled. "Are you okay or did you get some screws loose when you were underwater?"

With the mask still on his mouth, Robert stared at him and tried to speak, but only succeeded in stuttering incomprehensible words. The old millionaire tried to move closer.

"We did it," Robert whispered from behind the mask. "We did it!"

"Well, I can see you're not dead!" muttered Jack. "But what do you remember?"

Robert shook his head no. "No, Jack. *We* did it," he repeated before pulling the mask off his face. "I remember everything. My memory is back. I remember Patty. Our wedding day. Our first night together. Our first house. Every page of my books. Everything. Even these last few days when I was walking around in a daze—and you."

Jack stared at him in bewilderment. "Shit, man . . . really?"

Robert nodded affirmatively as he tried to get to his feet.

"And what did you think of the jump? Was it a success?"

"I think so. If I got my memory back, it's because the Robert Lewis from the other dimension went off to his own. Dead or alive. I think we were able to send him back to where he came from."

"Now, I'm the one who doesn't understand shit about this whole jumping thing," muttered Jack as he tried to get to his feet as well.

"My dear friend, I think there is little to understand. After all, this life — let's call it reality — is incomprehensible. We just must accept it the way it is. Yes, it's fine to struggle, but one must also accept the mysteries it sets before him. Now, could you please take me to the shore? I still have a wife, who I bet is upset she couldn't find me in bed this morning when she woke up and read that letter."

Jack beckoned his two young assistants to start the yacht engines. "But don't forget one thing, man!" he said.

"What, Jack?"

"You owe me a martini tonight."

The two smiled at each other as the boat slowly approached the harbor.

***

Once on mainland, Robert jumped into the first cab on the street. Excited, he yelled his address to the driver.

He finally remembered everything. All the things he had done in his life. From the plane ticket he had never used to the afternoon with Patty when they were planning their move into her parents' house. His decision not to leave. Their marriage, their travels, his books. Every single word he wrote.

He got out of the cab and ran to the front door with a pounding heart.

"Patty! Mosquito! Where are you?" He searched every room for his wife without getting any response.

In the kitchen, he saw that the letter he'd left her was missing. It could only mean that Patty had woken up and found it. Now she was no longer in the house. The idea of Patty being out there, distraught while looking for him, her husband, struck fear into him. He peered out the window, down in the direction of the beach. There she was. Sitting on the shoreline in the distance. Alone.

He smiled and ran out, flying down the steps leading to the beach.

Patty was staring at the horizon, lost in her tears, when he stopped behind her.

"Olive green," he blurted. Patty, bewildered, twisted to face him. "That's the color I wanted for our walls. Think about it! It wasn't a bad idea, after all."

Patty scrambled to her feet and flung her arms around him. "You finally remember!" she stammered, clinging tightly to his neck.

"Yes. I also remember that you do this wonderful whole roast fish with lemon and herbs and, since I'm starving, I think we'd better go back home and get to the oven. I'll help you."

Patty stared at him with a unique expression of shock, grief, and joy. "Sure! Whole roast fish . . . together."

Robert hugged her again. "We'll always do everything together from now on, mosquito."

"Of course, my love." Then she scowled playfully. "And after lunch, you'll tell me why you're soaked like a fish."

<h1 style="text-align:center">XXIII</h1>

**Laguna Beach 2022**

Robert and Patty walked along on the beach, hand in hand.

It had been four years since that night at the show in Los Angeles, four years since she had joined him at the hotel and they had made love and talked for a long time. They had seized the chance to build a new future, time they had thought they would never have together.

A few months later, when Patty's divorce was official, she went to live with Robert in his house in the Hamptons, outside New York. It had been four intense years spent trying to make up for all the lost time. While she continued to devote herself to painting, Robert had finished his first novel. He had written a love story — their story. The book had been published by one of the finest publishing houses in the world.

His dream had finally come true. He was reunited with Patty and could live on just doing what he always wanted to do: writing books. He didn't have to give up other important things in his life, either. Brian had graduated from Yale with top honors. He had been accepted into Stanford Law and would be starting in the fall. It was for that reason that after living for four years on the East Coast, Robert and Patty considered moving to California, where they could see Brian more often.

Which is what brought them to the steps of a house overlooking the ocean. It had large windows and a small terrace overlooking the coast, and a sign out front read "For Sale."

"This house is very similar to the one I dreamed about during my coma," Robert mused. "I remember us loving it in my dream. We would sit on the terrace and drink or dine in front of this spectacular ocean view."

Patty squeezed his hand even harder. "Then let's take it, my love," she replied with confidence.

Robert grinned and hugged her tightly. "Okay, let's talk about it over a glass of wine, a delicious fish dinner, and a nice view."

Patty smiled enthusiastically. "Where are you taking me?" she asked as she gently kissed his lips.

"I know a place nearby."

***

At The Cliff restaurant, Robert and Patty sat at a table overlooking the ocean.

"It's crazy," said Robert once he was seated in front of Patty. "It's exactly just like in my dream. It feels like I've been in this place for real!"

Patty took a sip of her Aperol Spritz. "What if it was one of those premonitory dreams? I've heard of it happening to other people, and I've read a lot about it. There are dreams that predict negative events. But maybe, in your case, it could have foretold you that something positive was about to happen . . . and we met again." As she spoke, she reached across the table and took Robert's hand.

"Maybe. Or maybe, while I was in a coma, I heard some doctor mentioned this place and, as it happened before to others, my mind created this story. Either way, I'm glad it all happened." He squeezed her hand. "No matter what, it brought you back to me. Only now I feel like a happy man."

They exchanged big smiles. They were staring at each other, basking in their love, when a waiter approached the table to take their orders. Robert chose grilled shrimp and a calamari salad. Patty opted for spaghetti with clams.

"I'm going to go to the bathroom for a minute, mosquito," he said playfully, after the waiter had walked away.

On his way to the restroom, he realized that he didn't need to ask for directions. This sudden thought made him cringe. Everything was weird and extremely real at the same time.

He looked at his reflection in the bathroom for a moment. It all felt like endless déjà vu. He had already dreamed about seeing that face in that mirror, his own worried face. Suddenly, his eyes were drawn to the painting on the wall next to him. It was a panorama of the Amalfi coast.

Robert felt petrified. Not only he was sure that he had seen that painting before, but he also remembered the vibes he had felt when it appeared in his dream years earlier. His legs felt suddenly weak. He laid his hands on the sink and tried to piece his memories together.

The whole thing had *not* been a dream. He really had taken "the leap." He had been in that bathroom before. In that life. Everything had *really* happened.

Justin York had been right—the Justin York who'd existed in that other dimension. The man who had explained what had happened to him was real. Alive. Somewhere else, in some other world, there was another Robert. Another Patty. Another Jack Redcliffe.

He splashed water over his face and hurried out of the bathroom. Patty was enjoying the view, cocktail in hand.

"It really happened," he blurted, making her jump. "It wasn't a dream! It's all real!"

"What do you mean, my love?" she asked, staring at him with confused eyes. "What's real?"

Robert sat in front of her and grabbed her hands. "It *wasn't* just a dream. I *really* did live in another dimension. I've seen it all before. The club, the view, the painting in the restroom."

"Robert, I don't understand what you're saying."

He breathed in through his nose and counted a few seconds before exhaling. He had to calm himself. "There's a painting in the restroom, an Italian landscape. I remember it. I remember seeing it in my . . . let's call them dreams. I remember it *precisely*. I also remember wondering if I had ever traveled. If I'd been to Italy. It wasn't a dream, Patty. You *must* believe me."

Patty's stunned expression rang a bell in his mind. He had already seen her looking at him like that. When he had disclosed Jack Redcliffe's theory to her in the other dimension, she thought he had gone insane.

He suddenly felt alone and scared. "Patty," he said firmly, "Please don't think I'm crazy. I can prove it to you."

She stared at him, confused and speechless. When she spoke, her voice was tense, but soft. "How do you intend to prove it to me, Robert?"

***

An hour later, they parked in front of the villa, the one he remembered as his own, and Robert and Patty got out of the car and went to ring the doorbell. After a few seconds, an elderly man appeared and asked who they were.

"Hello, my name is Robert Lewis, and I'm a writer. I wanted to ask if I could visit your home."

Dumbfounded, the man took his time before replying. "Why on earth would I let you visit my home?"

Promptly, Robert got into character. "Because we would like to make a movie based on my latest novel and this house, from the outside, looks just exactly what I had in mind for some scenes."

The old man seemed to consider for a few seconds. After all, such requests were not that unusual in California. Movies were shot all the time and all over the state.

"Well, I'm putting it up for sale anyway. I'm expecting a lot of visitors, as soon as I put the sign out. Be my guest." He moved away from the door to let the couple walk inside.

Robert had described the house to Patty in every detail on the drive over. Once they were inside, Patty gazed around in obvious shock. There was the kitchen. The terrace with a view of the beach. The bedroom. The walk-

230

in closet. The studio Robert had described meticulously, which the elderly owner was using as a small storage room. Everything was the same, down to the ceiling with its small skylights and the staircase that led down to the beach.

She was looking around, under Robert's eyes, as if she were experiencing a virtual reality, as if she had seen that place before.

Robert and Patty's eyes locked in a look a complicity, before he turned to the old man and asked, "Did you say you're going to put this house up for sale? For how much?"

# XXIV


**Sorrento, Italy, 2022**

Robert parked the rented Alfa Romeo convertible in front of a small black gate. He and Patty stepped out and stood still for a few seconds, one next to the other, staring at that entrance.

On the gate railing was a small copper plaque that read "Villa Maria."

"How do you plan to handle this, Robert?"

Robert remained silent, absorbed in one thought.

"Have you considered that she might think you're crazy?" she cautioned. "It took me a while to come around, and *I* love you, but a perfect stranger might call the police."

"All I know is that I have to do this. I made a promise," Robert said.

Patty grabbed his hand as a gesture of support. He looked at her and smiled, then rang the doorbell. After a few minutes, a young Asian woman emerged from the house and opened the gate. She was smiling at them.

"Mr. and Mrs. Lewis?" she asked.

Robert and Patty nodded.

"Mrs. Maria is waiting for you. Follow me," she said, as she led the way to the residence.

The mansion was surrounded by nature. Sculptures dotted all around the garden, among them an ancient amphora and a giant anchor eroded by water and time. The woman escorted them along the hallway of the villa up to a terrace overlooking a breathtaking view of the sea. On the horizon stood the majestic volcano, Vesuvius, overshadowing the ruins of Pompeii six miles away. The sight utterly absorbed Robert and Patty's attention.

"It's crazy, when I think about all the many coincidences," Robert breathed. "What we are looking at now is the same vista from that painting in the bathroom at The Cliff."

Patty smiled and nodded. A few minutes passed before an aged woman, accompanied by a young caregiver, appeared at the terrace glass door.

"Jack loved to dive into this sea," said the woman as she sat down in an armchair and beckoned them to do the same.

Robert and Patty approached her and gently shook her age-scarred hand.

"A pleasure to meet you, Mrs. Redcliffe," Robert said as he sat. "What a wonderful view you have here."

The woman nodded smilingly. "After Jack died, I decided this house was where I wanted to grow old, until my own departure from this world. I bought this mansion with my husband's insurance money, and I've been living here ever since. And it is here that I will wait for death to reunite me with my Jack." A nostalgic look entered her eyes. "Anyway, to what do I owe the pleasure of your visit? Mr. Lewis, you mentioned on the phone that it was something about Jack. What exactly can I do to help you?"

She peered at him with curious, lively eyes. Robert leaned forward, trying to get as close as possible to her so the words he was about to say would not be overheard. "Yes, Mrs. Maria. It's about your husband, Jack. And I don't know how to explain it to you without taking me for a fool or a delusional. I will try anyway."

Patty let out a deep, tense sigh. Robert knew how difficult this moment was for both of them, how complicated it would be to explain to the widow what he had experienced, seen, and heard. Patty had chosen to believe him and to stand by his side.

Robert began to speak in one breath. He had had his speech prepared for quite a long time. Hours passed and the sun came down to touch the horizon, painting the sky crimson. The volcano, which had been dormant for centuries, was now changing tint, creating a dark shadow that overlooked the entire valley.

Robert told the old woman about his accident. His coma. His dream. About waking up in Laguna Beach. He spoke about Patty and the memory of her. He finally got to his meeting with Jack Redcliffe, how he got lost in his memories. He told her about his love for her, Maria, the same woman who now sat in front of him.

He explained Justin York's theory of "the leap" and how Jack helped him in plunging into the icy waters of the Pacific at dawn four years earlier, in a dimension that was different from the one they were experiencing in that very moment.

Jack's widow remained silent for as long as he spoke, without ever diverting her gaze from him. Tears ran down her careworn face when Robert told her about the love her husband had felt for her, about how alone he had felt with nothing but the memory of her. About his devotion to the woman who was lost in another world, far away, somewhere else in the universe.

Finally Robert said, "Before I dived into the sea, Jack made me promise that I would deliver his message to you."

The woman nodded and waited to hear what Robert had to reveal to her.

"Jack asked me to come find you and tell you that he still loves you. And that he will love you forever, wherever you are, no matter in what corner of the universe you were. He made me promise to do so, and now . . ."

Her whisper interrupted. "So, that man was you."

Robert looked at her, confused and intrigued at the same time.

Even Patty, who up to that moment had remained silent on the sidelines, bounced with excitement in the armchair she had been sitting on.

"I don't understand. What do you mean?" asked Robert.

Maria shifted her eyes from Robert to the horizon, where the sun was on the verge of sinking into the sea. "I've been dreaming of Jack since the day he died at least once a week. Often several times a week, I would fall asleep and see him. I would see him sad. Lost. He would ask for my help. Sometimes in a desperate way. But there was a time when, suddenly, in my dreams, he started showing up with a different mood. He was smiling. Happy. Not resigned but fulfilled instead."

As she spoke, the woman interrupted herself to wipe her cheeks with the cloth handkerchief she had been holding since the beginning of their visit, and which was now soaked with tears. "One night he appeared while he was on a beach. There was someone with him. A man. A man I didn't recognize because everything looked blur. That's why I didn't recognize you right away. That man was you."

Robert's eyes widened. He didn't dare stop the woman from speaking.

"Jack was smiling. He had renewed vigor. I always thought he was appearing in my dream from the beyond. Some sort of heaven. He was still connected, still in communication with me. That was the only explanation I had for what I was experiencing."

She fell silent for a little while, under Robert and Patty's watchful eyes. Perhaps she was trying to find the right words to explain what she was feeling in that moment.

She turned and stared at Robert intently, clearing her throat. "Thank you, Mr. Lewis. Thank you for having the courage to share this with me. Now I know. I believe you. Thank you for what you did for Jack, because wherever he is at this moment, universes or worlds away, his life has begun to make sense. I can feel it."

Patty's eyes welled with tears. Robert, too, couldn't hide the one sliding down his face. There was a silence under the darkening sky. Streetlamps flickered on, illuminating the house perched on the coast.

They had just barely driven away from the villa when Robert parked his car on the side of the street. He turned off the engine and sat silent, gazing at the nighttime panorama of the coastline.

"Are you okay, my love?" Patty asked.

He clutched the steering wheel tightly in his hands, sighed, and turned his eyes to her. "Everything Justin York said is true. But there is much more. It is true that different dimensions intertwine. They overlap as they travel. But he couldn't tell for how much. Every time we think we know someone we've never met before. Every time we have a déjà vu. Every time we find ourselves in a place that feels familiar. That we wake up happy or sad without knowing the reason. That we dream of something incomprehensible or to which we cannot give a rational explanation. Each time we have what we believe to be an illumination, a strange vibe or sensation. All of this happens because our life in this dimension overlaps others for a moment. Unconsciously, we send ourselves signals from one part of the universe to another. People we know or love, and who are in different realities, do the same with us. *Everything* is connected. *Everything* makes sense. Coincidences do not exist. We have so much yet to discover in this world. So much to explain."

Patty gave a hint of a smile. Robert wasn't crazy, and by the love shining in her eyes, he knew he had proven it to her.

"That Robert from the other dimension felt and experienced my sadness in this life. And that, without his knowing it, was why he felt the need to attend one of Justin York's conferences. Because in some way he could feel *my* need, *my* lack of fulfillment in his dimension, and couldn't understand why. When I had the accident and thought regretfully of you, that connection made the two dimensions overlap."

"Robert, do you think you're the only person that has discovered how the dimensions are so connected?" Patty asked.

Robert threw his head back for just a moment. "I don't know, but I intend to find out," he concluded and started the engine.


THE END

Other Book by the Author:

The Sicilian Detective (2010)
Conspiracy of Silence (2019)
Girl in a Glass Box (2023)